SENTENCE

.II.

PRAISE FOR MIKHAIL IOSSEL

Sentence
LLP 2025

Mikhail Iossel has created a genre of his own—a mix of memoir, speculative fiction, philosophical reflection–and a flavoured language distinctly his, highly lyrical and melodic; Iossel is a sort of linguistic Paganini, delivering capriccios with a playful joy, and occasionally he decelerates in a melancholy way as he nostalgically reminisces about the passage of time, death, and his former life in the Soviet Union.

—Josip Novakovich, author of *Rubble of Rubles*

These one-sentence stories, some lasting only a moment, others zipping thrillingly through years and continents, tap deep into childhood, old age, friendship, memory, dislocation, and the act of writing itself—in other words, this messy, beautiful mortal life to which we have all been sentenced. They are also, in the face of every refusal, funny and tender, and suffused with hope. Mikhail Iossel is one of the most innovative writers of our time.

—Dawn Raffel, author of *Boundless as the Sky*

Sentence is a brilliant and breathless literary manifestation of speed that made me think of Gogol and the prose of Blaise Cendrars in his fictional trip on the Trans-Siberian express. Here, a brooding Russian Jew vividly recalls his Soviet childhood in a cramped communal apartment and the subsequent many losses he has experienced, ones that flash by like the view through the window of a fast train. Iossel's narrator is moving and melancholy, insightful and aphoristic and unlike anyone else you are likely to read in contemporary writing.

—Antanas Sileika, author of *The Death of Tony*

When Mikhail Iossel emigrated to the United States at 30, the sentence offered him a kind of refuge, a means to grasp the English language. Now the sentence offers him something more profound: a doorway into memory, and the past he left behind. *Sentence* is a true original; an extraordinary stroll, line by line, through the mind of one of our most joyful, erudite, and innovative writers. Every writer should read this book.

—Jessica Anthony, author of *The Most*

Mikhail Iossel is one of our greatest contemporary writers. He carries the torch of Russian literary genius, writing with brilliance of the snake pit of Soviet Communism. His gift for characterization, vivid imagery and absurdity makes his work mesmerizing. His writing is unforgettable.

—David Evanier, author of *Red Love*

Love Like Water, Love Like Fire
Winner, 2023 QWF Hugh MacLennan Prize for Fiction

What distinguishes Iossel as a writer, aside from his obvious talent for atmospheric dramedy, is his lucid, musical prose style. . . Iossel's marvelous sense of rhythm dazzles the reader. We can't stop turning the pages of this book.

—*New York Times Book Review*

Harrowing, hilarious, dark, and devastating. . . Iossel's sentences twist the reader through the illogical forces of dictatorship, childhood, puberty, survival, and writing angsty poetry in a communist regime.

—*Paragraphe Hugh MacLennan Prize jury citation*

The former USSR continues to cast a long shadow on our current affairs, but Mikhail Iossel brings a fresh eye to the region. . . Engaging equally with the absurdity and brutality of life in a repressive regime, [*Love Like Water, Love Like Fire* is] perfect for fans of Gogol and George Saunders alike.

—*Chicago Review of Books*

Very funny. . . In *Love like Water, Love like Fire*, jokes point to the absurdities and logical contradictions in everyday life. . . There is something refreshing about Iossel's willingness to maintain his sense of irony, even about such intractable subjects as anti-Semitism, the ghastliness of Soviet bureaucracy, or the irreconcilability of death with human happiness.

—*Literary Review of Canada*

Iossel is an exception among the writers of his generation. . . Full of subtle irony and macabre humour, his prose makes such skillful use of American colloquialism that it is as though these stories take place in some fictional Soviet-America.

—*Times Literary Supplement*

Honest and compassionate. If there's one takeaway from *Love Like Water, Love Like Fire*, it's that this compassion may be necessary today more than ever.

—*Winnipeg Free Press*

Brilliant. [Iossel] has created a style that is as intriguing and richly suggestive as that of his predecessor, Vladimir Nabokov.

—*Canberra Times*

An expertly written set of stories, often brimming with dark humour, offering many vantage points from which to consider the Soviet experience, and the particular burdens it placed on Jews.

—*J. The Jewish News of Northern California*

Iossel brings his warm, gently ironic authorial voice to bear on the cruel and often surreal lives of Jews in the Soviet Union... 'There is love like fire, and there is love like water,' say the Hasidic masters, and Iossel's collection explores that dichotomy.

—*Jewish Book Council*

[A] vibrant collection... With an ear for the clumsiness of Russian bureaucratic nomenclature, an eye for Kafkaesque humiliations, and a heart that embraces all the paradoxes of being a Soviet Jew, Iossel casts a spell over the reader. Reading like Sholem Aleichem updated by Bruce Jay Friedman, these stories reflect the exciting evolution of Russian Jewish literature.

—*Publishers Weekly*

[An] engaging collection... While many stories illuminate the absurdity of Soviet society, Iossel conveys the brutal oppression of the surveillance state most intensely, and hauntingly, in the title story.

—*Kirkus Reviews*

Replete with an erudite wit and eloquent wisdom, *Love Like Water, Love Like Fire* is an extraordinary, thoughtful, and thought-provoking read.

—*Midwest Book Review*

Love Like Water, Love Like Fire is an extraordinary book: funny and profound, moving and provocative. Rarely has life in the former USSR (or anywhere, for that matter) been portrayed with such a rich admixture of soaring observation and finely rendered detail. This is a gorgeously constructed collection by one of our wittiest and most insightful writers.

—Molly Antopol, author of *The UnAmericans*

Iossel is a genius, a comic visionary in the tradition of Gogol, Keret, Barthelme, and Saunders. *Love Like Water, Love Like Fire* is a book of surprises and delights.

—Brian Morton, author of *Starting Out in the Evening, Florence Gordon*

Dark and funny. . . [Iossel's stories] provide an insider's take on what it's like to survive in a terrifying yet absurd reality.

—Sharon Weinberg, *Chatham Bookstore (Chatham, NY) on WAMC The Roundtable*

SENTENCE

stories

MIKHAIL IOSSEL

Editor: Linda Leith
Cover image: Mikhail Iossel
Cover design: Debbie Geltner
Author photo: Douglas Anthony Cooper

Library and Archives Canada Cataloguing in Publication

Title: Sentence : stories / Mikhail Iossel.
Names: Iossel, Mikhail, author
Identifiers: Canadiana (print) 20240540387 | Canadiana (ebook) 20240540395 | ISBN 9781773901749 (softcover) | ISBN 9781773901756 (EPUB) | ISBN 9781773901763 (PDF)
Subjects: LCGFT: Short stories.
Classification: LCC PS8617.O87 S46 2025 | DDC C813/.54Edidc23

Printed and bound in Canada.

The publisher gratefully acknowledges the support of the Government of Canada through the Canada Council for the Arts, the Canada Book Fund, and of the Government of Quebec through the Société de développement des entreprises culturelles (SODEC).

Linda Leith Publishing
Montreal
www.lindaleith.com

TO THE MEMORY OF ROBERT COOVER, BAKHYT KENJEEV,
STAN PERSKY, AND ALEXEI TSVETKOV

"All I can come up with are stray sentences, he said,
maybe because reality seems to me
like a swarm of stray sentences."

—Roberto Bolaño, *Antwerp,*
translated by Natasha Wimmer

"...with every hour spent alone,
with every sentence that you draft,
you win back a piece of your life."

—Elias Canetti, *The Book Against Death*
translated by Peter Filkins

SENTENTIA LONGA, FABULA BREVIS

Table of Contents

1

DMD

On January 9, 1986 (I would remember the date because, of course, it was the Bloody Sunday of 1905, that of the ubiquitous mentions in Soviet school history books), less than two weeks before leaving the Soviet Union for good, for the first and last time in my life (the Soviet Union — not Russia), I was returning to Leningrad from Moscow, also for the last time ever (Leningrad — not St. Petersburg), after three strange (and of course, everything felt eerily strange to me at that juncture in my life), shapelessly endless booze-fueled days and nights of bidding incoherent funereal farewells to a motley crowd of friends and acquaintances there, in the giant stone heart of the eternal Soviet golem, on an unexpectedly (but then, again, it was the middle of the first work week of the New Year, and the increasingly dispirited giant country was still dawdling in glum post-holiday lethargy, all across its senseless eleven time zones) half-empty Red Arrow, once the famously upscale train for the so-called Soviet elites (not the right word, I know, but it would be boring, both for you and for me, if I were to say instead something along the lines of "the transiently lucky and generally pitiful servants and beneficiaries of an irredeemably ugly totalitarian regime") connecting Russia's former and present capitals, the respective avatars of its hopeless European aspirations and its shambolic Scythian essence, and invariably departing from either point at five minutes to midnight (from Leningrad's Moskovsky train station, it did so to the diffusely loud accompaniment of Reinhold Gliere's "Hymn to the Great City — the finale of his famous ballet "The Bronze Horseman," but — not that it matters any, and silence has always suited me just fine — I don't recall any such acoustic reciprocity on the part of the Leningradsky train station in Moscow); and the only other passenger sharing the standard four-bunk compartment with me that night, my compartment-mate and fellow-traveller (yes, I am aware that this term has a different meaning in modern Western parlance… to pre-empt your possible impulse to explain this to me), was a stoop-shouldered tall man with intense deep-set and as though inward-staring eyes (this is putting it perhaps a bit too fancily, I concur, but what can I do if that actually was my first impression of him) and eagle's-beak of a nose (agreed: a cliché, and a fairly insipid one at that, by implication — although, of course, I am Jewish myself, so… so nothing, actually), appearing to be in his mid-seventies (later on, he turned out to be sixty-five; close enough, although I certainly was not a good judge of people's age at the time… still am not) and bearing a certain overall resemblance to the great Soviet stage and film actor Rostislav Plyatt in the hallmark role of Pastor Schlag in the timeless television series "Seventeen Moments of Spring," who slouched in obliquely through the heavy sliding compartment door less than a minute before the train had taken off with a protracted trembling in slanted driving snow (but was it actually snowing in Moscow that night… I'm not sure, although I seem to remember so, but… let me not waste our shared time here on trying to say something interesting about that) and, as though by way of an excessively and indeed too aggressively friendly wordless introduction, in an almost defiant gesture, produced from his beat-up black cardboard suitcase (yes, the classic old Soviet-style one) and placed with a thud (three thuds of varying loudness, to be accurate) on the small console table by the window, two bottles of the exclusive and strictly *defitsitnyi* five-star Armenian "Ararat" cognac (that last word applied to any kind of brandy in the old Soviet Union… another tidbit of useless information for you) and a large box of what shortly thereafter would be revealed to be the delicious chocolate-covered Estonian pralines, called Maiuspala (the box's unbearably pretty halcyon-blue cover featured a supernaturally blond little girl gazing lovingly at a few intensely yellow and irresistibly cute fluffy little chicks); and since (it's a commonly known fact) nothing can bring random travellers through the night close together faster than two bottles of brandy chased with chocolates (and because, obviously, it would've been churlish and rude and, well, downright stupid of me to decline his unexpected lavish offerings), we got right down to it, drinking and eating, talking animatedly and, in all, quickly forming a deceptively strong bond of nascent open-ended friendship, in the good old literary and cinematic and generically Russian (true that) manner of two strangers sharing a compartment on a night train and getting drunk (wasted would be a more expressive word) together and revealing (as they say in self-help literature) to each other the most essential truths of their respective existences; and thus, after our first approximately one- or two-hundred grams per liver (consumed from two heavy thick-faceted railroad glasses, separated for some reason from their ubiquitous and comfortingly familiar Stalinist silver-bronze glass-holders and brought over, as per our request, by the sullen and likely residually hungover trainwoman — who informed us, entirely unbidden and in a whiny, peevish tone, that if we wanted tea, too, we were plumb out of luck, due to the hot water tank in the carriage not quite being sufficiently hot, owing, in turn, to the insufficient quantity and subpar quality of the coal at her disposal… thanks, as she went on to remark completely out of the blue, to "that devil-marked Gorbachev of yours," which outrageous and provocative statement, potentially an entrapment attempt, although of course not, was taken perfectly in stride by the two of us, my compartment-mate and I, as we just shrugged our shoulders and rolled our eyes, frowned a little and said nothing to her in response), I learned from him that he was a widower of three years' standing (his wife, to whom by the time of her death, he'd been married for over three decades, just didn't wake up, failed to open her eyes one morning, for no clear health-related reason) and a retired senior accountant at Leningrad's largest regional concrete-distribution centre (not an exciting job, my friend, by any stretch of the imagination, he remarked with a chuckle, I'll grant you that, but still a pretty important one), while about me, in turn, he got to find out that I'd been trained as an electromagnetic engineer in college (submarine demagnetization, all that arcane stuff) and had worked in junior engineer's capacity afterwards, for a couple of years, at an appropriately profiled secret-research institute (a PO Box, yes... we both kind of winked at each other with exaggerated mock-seriousness, and he also nodded and brought a knobbly yellow finger to his bloodless bluish lips, to indicate that he knew how to keep a secret, mum as a grave — and we both laughed), but for the past five... yes, and a half years had been a shift security guard in the Roller-Coaster Unit of the Amusement Sector at the Central Park of Culture and Leisure (again my compartment-mate nodded knowingly, sagely, with a subtle smile, observing that he could easily fathom as to what concrete practical or existential circumstances such a sudden and sharp career change could have been precipitated or necessitated by), plus I also and primarily was an underground, samizdat writer, I informed him, a tad too self-importantly (and instantly disliking myself for that), in an archly, starchy meaningful tone of someone keenly aware that he hasn't written anything remotely notable or genuinely good yet and is not at all certain he ever would (and of course, right away, he wanted to know what it was, in general, that I wrote about... oh, life and death, I told him, and everything in-between — and we both laughed again); and then, after our second refill of our glasses, he let me know (and it came as a shock to me, of course) that just recently, only about two and a half weeks earlier (he mentioned the exact date, and I started involuntarily, for it was my father's birthday), my compartment-mate or fellow-traveller or drinking companion or whatever (it's high time I started referring to him by a specific name of some kind, or an acronym maybe — DMD, for instance, Dead Man Drinking, why not), was diagnosed with inoperable brain cancer and given three-to-four months to live, by a refreshingly sympathetic young doctor (whose last name was something like... well, it started with Che... Che... Che-something... no, not Che Burashka, haha, well, unfortunately, forgetting more and more things lately — words, names, you name it... by the day, if not hour) at that oncological clinic over on the Liteyny, close by the Big House (you must know the Big House, something is telling me — and I just closed and opened my eyes in the affirmative, yeah, did I ever), and so this quick trip to Moscow he was returning from now, at the same time with me, coincidentally, for the very last time in his life (and that last circumstance, sadly or not, was a dead certainty now) had been undertaken on his silly, fussy, excessively death-fearing sister-in-law's relentless pestering insistence, in a last-ditch effort to... well, cheat death, one supposed (although he really didn't mind dying all that much, seriously, he really did not, what the hell was the big deal, he'd lived a sufficiently long life and... well, and so on, stuff too boring, in the existential context of our Soviet lives, even to discuss), in order to be seen (again, through selfsame sister-in-law's murky connections in that nebulous netherworld of homeo-paganistic quasi-medical folk-quackery) by some fabled underground miracle-worker of a cancer-curer, the supposedly legendary and mysterious cancer-whisperer (such embarrassingly stupid nonsense really) who ran a clandestine (no kidding) and officially nonexistent (well, obviously) private practice at random nighttime hours in a rambling wooden cabin on the outskirts of Balashikha (a distant suburb of Moscow... explained I helpfully, you're welcome), and who, upon the rather perfunctory and more than a little odd (aural or palpatory, if those are the words... incantatory maybe — there certainly was quite a bit of liturgical-like, churchy kind of mumbling involved) examination of DMD, had shaken his oddly shaped head with a heavy sigh (face concealed by full-length red cloth mask, incidentally — such a dramatic creep) and told DMD, in a voice both rueful and businesslike, that, much to his great regret, there was nothing that could be done anymore, not by him and therefore certainly not by anyone else, very sadly indeed, as the disease had already spread through and taken an irreversible hold of every vital focal point and what have you in its host's body, so, in short, again, yes, too late, too late (so very irritating it was, that sadistic fake sympathy, let me tell you, what exactly was it that was too late, it's never too late to freaking die, that's for sure... but at least that sanctimonious charlatan had the basic decency to return half of the five-hundred-ruble deposit received by him in advance, in addition to turning down as too-frivolous, yes, that pious prick, the offering of this here cognac and chocolates); and I... well, as you can imagine, I was taken aback, spooked (if that's the word) more than a little, I admit, when he imparted to me that information (and in truth, wouldn't you be also, um, unnerved, if on the threshold of starting a whole new life in a new world it had suddenly developed that you would be spending the night in an inescapably tight enclosed space with, and telling all kinds of personal stuff about yourself to, an incurably sick, dying man, while getting drunk with him... something Shakespearean or, you know, Bergmanesque about the whole setup, definitely not a good omen), and I told him, of course, reflexively, that, obviously, I was very sorry to hear that, so incredibly sorry, of course, oh man, so very sorry, so-so… and cutting me off with a scowling, dark look on his face, he told me to knock it off forthwith, for if I didn't, he'd smash this here cognac bottle, an almost empty one already, true enough, but still, a bottle is a damn bottle, over my freaking stupid head with his full remaining force, seeing that he'd already made it very clear to me that he was not afraid to die, not freaking afraid, and was actually looking forward to it, to no longer existing, if I wanted to know the truth, yes, seriously, not being coy or, like, coquettish or anything here, so… so fair enough, acknowledging his forcefully made point with a slight incline of my increasingly heavy, echoing head, I confided in him then (and please understand that doing so represented a qualitatively different leap of faith on my part, since… well, this still was the freaking Soviet Union and I didn't know him at all, this man, who could've lied to me about his brain cancer and all that, and who actually could've been a KGB provocateur or some such, sent in to derail my departure for America and ruin my whole freaking life, so yeah, it was a plunge in the dark for me) that thanks to Gorbachev and his urgent, financially motivated dire need to improve his relations with the West, in less than two weeks I would be leaving the Soviet Union for good, along probably with thousands of other refuseniks from across the country, yes indeed, I know, man, thanks, yes, after more than five freaking years of being a freaking refusenik (and DMD, beaming, slapped me on the shoulder at that, and guffawed, saying he'd known from the very first, as soon as he'd laid eyes on me upon entering the compartment, that I was a fellow aidishe boy, well, mazeltov, and… oh, how funny and strangely and happily coincidental, or serendipitous, whatever the word, it really was that, hey, here we were, in the same train compartment on the same night, two Soviet Jews imminently about to escape the freaking Soviet Union for good, if admittedly in two slightly different ways, by two different routes, two alternate modes of dying — one real and the other, um, more metaphorical, although still pretty damn real), as the two of us were careening, if that's the word, through the boundless wintry Soviet night, with its immeasurable darkness, for the very last time in our respective Soviet lives, the thought of which had made me both extremely and almost unbearably excited, but also scared as hell, full of uncertainty and tre… trep… trepidation (and DMD told me, hiccupping, that was more than absolutely understandable, my feelings were at the moment, because death, taken as a freaking datum — say what — was a damn riddle wrapped in a mystery inside an enema, to quote Churchill); and then, with my head spinning slowly, I also told him, almost despite myself, that… yes, that… on a different yet adjacent subject, that my father and I, we'd just barely begun to be back on speaking terms with each other, after all this time, all these years of total non-communication, the pointedly surly mutual avoidance — with my poor mother being torn between the two of us — because of his, my father's, justifiable, I'll admit that, resentment at my having gone ahead, autonomously, on my own, albeit after years of duly forewarning him and my mother (but he just wouldn't take those warnings seriously), and applying for an exit visa… which, again (again and again, OK, dad), was a pretty egotistical move on my part, objectively speaking, yes, objectively (but there's no any essential truth in objectivity), so it was no wonder he felt mortally wounded in his feelings, in addition to being morally indignant, so much so that he'd refused outright to provide me with his crucially essential official consent to my leaving the freaking Soviet Union for good, refused to sign the official paper stating in effect that he didn't mind his son's effectively becoming a traitor to the freaking motherland, thereby automatically, like, making a refusenik out of me, you know, by that refusal of his (too cute by half, that turn of phrase, I know), and I couldn't really blame him for this, either, looking back, like I already said, especially in light of the fact that as an inevitable and immediate result of my application, he was stripped of his top-level security clearance and all that… stuff necessary for him to, you know, possess in order to continue being one of the leading freaking designers of our hopelessly outmoded Soviet submarines' electromagnetic defences, yes, and… and moreover, to my intense lingering subsequent latent shame (one or more of these adjectives here is superfluous and must go, but… OK, not right now, later), at one point, shortly after he'd refused to grant me that official consent, I, filled with seething anger and the unbearably smug and downright repugnant youthful arrogance as I was, given the intensity of the situation, I told my father, more or less in those very words, verbatim practically, that he'd already had his chance to live his life to the fullness of its (admittedly, limited, in the Stalinist USSR) potential, his life's cruelly truncated promise, and that the bulk of his life had already been behind him, lived out, not to mince… yeah, and to think that he was so much younger then than I am now, too, reader… so now, I told my father, it was my time to experience life, to chart my own path in it, while for him it was time to step aside, stop being egotistical, to set me free, as any loving father would, to liberate me (yes, I actually said that) to live my life the way I wanted and where I wanted to live it, which most definitely was not in the Soviet Union, no, definitely not, but in a different world, in a… well, in an infinitely broader one, father, enough was enough, I said to him, Stalin had long been dead even as a metaphor, even as a metaphor's shadow, a hieroglyph of humiliating deadly fear, and there no longer was any latent Soviet fear bred in my brittle post-Stalinist bones, so let me be, dad, don't laugh, I want to be a free writer in a free world (don't laugh, dad), rather than yet another joyless Soviet engineer, submarine demagnetizer, no matter how maybe nominally accomplished or not… oh, DMD, how guilty, let me tell you, I felt afterwards, how sickened by my own cruelty, how contemptible, deplorable I had revealed myself to myself to be, what a fool, such a damn bastard, I was almost crying at that point, with an equally drunk and indeed quite pale and gaunt DMD looking on silently, sympathetically, at me slumped forward across that small console table between us, my face but a few centimetres from his, as the two of us were rolling, rollicking along with the Red Arrow express train, travelling through night's all-encompassing darkness, the two superfluous, superannuated (not sure what that word means, but I like the sound of it) lambs of god (oh God), two human silhouettes bent toward each other over the small console table by the train window, glasses in their hands, inside the stark frame of darkly yellow light, as we already were approaching Bologoye — the small town (is it even an actual place… no question mark, a rhetorical question) smack in the middle of the train's distance between Russia's two capitals — the Red Arrow slowing down, coming to a stop gradually, haltingly, with a shudder, sighing tiredly, with the dull, staid grey-yellow light of the station's lanterns mingling unsuccessfully with the intense, harsh yellow brightness inside our compartment, and we already were more than halfway through the second bottle of that five-star pseudo-cognac, too, the dusky placid light of the Bologoye train station reminding us (oh, just speak for yourself) of the memories of our own lives, much of which latter we, like most other people in this world, hadn't been able to retain all too well, holding on to very few of them actually, hardly any at all, dispiritingly enough, as if our own lives had happened to some other people, rather than the only us ever to exist in the world, oh, such a dolorous thought, such a terrible waste of a perfectly good lifetime, you know, so we were legitimately sad at that moment, paused in the night in Bologoye, with me still crying quietly, sniffling spasmodically and gradually calming down, while DMD kept telling me again (but actually, just speaking to himself, sotto voce, mumbling as though in a trance, shaking his head mulishly now and then) that he was not afraid to die, not afraid, and not sorry about anything, nothing at all, definitely not sorry about never getting to see the shitty big wide world out there, this time around on this planet, all those New

York-Paris-London-Rio places and so on, the whole freaking non-Soviet world, or even much of the Soviet one, either, obviously, so incomprehensibly gigantic, well, see, because his life, the one coming to an end now, it hadn't been about that, this time around, not about travelling and, like, the expanding or deepening of itself or… being interesting or fulfilling, which was all right by him, for one doesn't get to choose the time and place or other basic elements of one's life's essential parameters and… so on, all that self-excusing claptrap, so he simply (easier said than done, of course) would have to live a much more, like, interesting, intense, rewarding and fulfilling and joyous life the next time around, you know, when he got his chance to be reborn, when his time for that would come, his turn, which he had no other recourse but totally to believe was absolutely freaking going to happen, him returning to this world as someone else, unbeknownst to himself, as a clean slate of a human, to this future and barely recognizable world of ours (curiosity is the only factor making me regretful about this whole dying thing, my friend), yes, hopefully as a human being again, rather than, say, a monitor lizard or a hyena, which he thought he stood a pretty good chance at, being reborn as a human, since he didn't believe, didn't think honestly that he had committed any really grave, serious, cardinal, like, sins and all that in this, current life of his, which was now rapidly rolling toward its end, except, well… yeah, well (and he gave me a pleading, tortured look, his eyes heavy with pain), OK, here goes, except for cheating on his wife with another woman while his wife was still alive, there, he said it, yes, another woman, whom he'd been seeing, as the phrase has it, for nine years and four months by now, by this final juncture of his freaking journey, and with whom he still was very much in love, sappy as that may sound, so feel free to laugh (while I was still crying quietly, while listening — laughing at him just then would've been the last thought on my mind), which fact, that love, constituted the ultimate truth and both the greatest sin and the utmost joy of his life, he went on, although obviously he was not a religious man, for what was there even to be religious about in this damn country of ours, what was sin to begin with, just a word, a silly word that didn't apply to love, or maybe it did, what did he know, since he personally felt his love for the woman who'd never been his wife, while his wife still had been alive, was a sin, or might have been, both his happiness and his curse, and if it was a sin then he regretted it, although he still loved her very much, that woman, now more than ever, even as we were speaking now, he freaking loved her, and it was a shame, he said, also beginning to cry, a damn shame that he would have to leave her so soon now, alone in this world, but oh well, enough of this maudlin nonsense, he would miss her very much in his eternal nonexistence, and she would be miserable without him in the world also, although maybe not, oh well, yes, who could tell, life was life, so what could he do, a sin was a sin (and he smiled a little, as he sang that out in an unmelodic voice, "you must remember this, a sin was still a sin," although of course not, for how would he know the lyrics of an American golden oldie), yes, breaking his late wife's heart probably was a sin, definitely, for she must've sensed something… and perhaps, and even very likely, that might have been one of the big reasons she'd refused, you know, to wake up that awful (yet also liberating, one supposed) morning three years ago, had chosen to die, cease to exist, rather than… and that was a shame, but what could one do, what could he have done differently, love was love, it was not a sin, enough of this boring maudlin shite, life was life, love was love, a reason unto itself, so hopefully his having been in love with another woman for all these years would not in the end be counted against him, in the context of, you know, preventing him from being reborn as a human being at some future point in eternity, rather than a cobra, for instance, although cobras didn't know they were cobras and therefore led a pretty untroubled emotional existence… or maybe, my friend, there might be another possibility (and he perked up a bit and lifted his head higher and looked at me coyly from his swimming eyes), his body alone would die, just his body, if die it must, which it did have to, inevitably, but his soul, his sac…uh… rosant inner being, well, what if it just refused to expire along with its mortal chamber, just freaking refused to do so, to comply, yeah, screw that, screw death, and so his spirit would then move on conceivably and enter and proceed to inhabit someone else's body — yours, my young friend, he said to me, winking, why not, yes, yours, in freaking America, for there were no distances too great for one's spirit, and we both laughed, while still crying a little, two dead men alive and drinking, sitting on our corporeal butts on our rigid lower bunks in our Red Arrow compartment, travelling through the dark, two imminently dying men, one old, one young, although, literally, technically speaking, only one of us was actually actively dying, dying on an accelerated schedule, while the other was doing so, um, more metaphorically, in literary terms only, which still meant literally (metaphorically speaking… no, it didn't), since my leaving the Soviet Union for good, as an emigré, as a figurative (oh, stop it) traitor to the motherland, meant in terms starkly practical that I would never see my loved ones again, my family, my friends, you name it, even those I didn't particularly like, no matter, because treason (even if only a figurative one) was generally punishable by death everywhere (merely speaking figuratively, yes… oh, shut up), and so I would be dead effectively, figuratively, and they would never see me again, my loved and unloved ones alike, since I would never be allowed to return, and no one from this Soviet world would ever be allowed either to travel to where I would dwell in my post-Soviet netherworld…. my unreachable nevermore of the ultimate capitalist abroad of unimaginable America, which meant, simply put, that the morning of seeing me off at the airport, for those who'd come to see me off there, to bid me an eternal farewell and… stuff, would in essence be one of burying me, metaphorically but also kind of literally, too, in their hearts and minds — so yes, it would be the morning of my funeral, for them, as well as for me, speaking metaphorically (time to let go of that freaking adverb already), so emigration was indeed death, I told DMD, only the kind of one where you died and then still continued to go on living; and so… so nothing, it was so dark outside, so hopelessly and eternally dark, and so… and so nothing; and I also remember telling him then, the quietly weeping DMD, how (but wait, no — how could I have been telling him about something that would only take place in my American future, no matter how imminent, which hadn't happened yet… I was drunk, sure, but not prophetic) — yes, how, never mind, how, soon after arriving in America, not more than a month maybe into my second life (ooh, his second life, wow, such a momentous development for the entire freaking world, you self-important prick), my post-Soviet existence (I was living then in an enormously-sized but poorly laid-out apartment with lots of rooms on both sides of a long sinuous corridor, not entirely unlike the communal apartment of my early childhood in midtown Leningrad, in a rambling, rumbling, slum-like rooftop apartment in a dilapidated flophouse in Brookline, Massachusetts, owned by a fellow Soviet-Jewish immigrant, bald and cunning and shifty-eyed and cheerily talkative, and inhabited by seven young and likely undocumented Colombians, who worked on a construction site in downtown Boston and kept a bunch of piranhas in a massive tank in the living room, plus a highly sophisticated Lithuanian theatre director, who spoke native-quality Russian and perfect English), well, in short, in really short order I developed a bad case of agoraphobia, the irrational fear of open spaces, an offshoot of depression, obviously, raging anxiety, PTSD, the whole enchilada; and as a result I was fired from my first American job, that of an information-desk clerk at a tony bookstore in Harvard Square (I just couldn't make my vertiginous, nauseated, altogether pathetic, semi-suicidal self to get itself on downtown-bound T train to get there, to that bookstore, plus my English admittedly was inadequate to the store's exacting standards, and there'd be days when I went without food altogether, unable as I was to force myself to step out to the supermarket across the street, and oh, my heart, how many days and nights had I spent there, in my tiny room in that terrible cruel apartment, prone on my back on my narrow sagging bed in the corner, under the hellishly hot tin roof of that dilapidated flophouse, and listening to the seven Colombians' piranha-cheering shouts in the living room, as well as the insanely agitated, husky, raspy voice of the Boston Celtics' TV announcer, that crazy Johnny Most guy, coming from my black-and-white portable TV with rabbit ears that only could catch one channel, the Boston Celtics one, and thinking that if the old push were to come to the ultimate shove of its logical conclusion, well, as long as there was death there was hope — a very comforting, heart-warming thought, let me tell you… but don't try it at home); and how, then, one day (just get on with the story already… what story), trembling like a leaf (what kind of leaf, be specific... fine, an aspen one), I walked out of the house, into the simmering open space, in a desperate effort to overcome my shameful inner brokenness, hating and despising myself and my pathetic invisible surreal illness, to try and prove it to myself that that freaking fear of open spaces was all in my head, in my imagination, for crying out loud, enough already, I kept telling myself, to no avail; be a man, be a goddamn man, get a hold of yourself, get a grip… and so I dragged myself, dying inwardly with every single step, to Harvard Circle, just a couple of short blocks away, and then walked a few metres past it, beyond the T line, at which point, feeling totally exhausted, I sat heavily on a lonesome lopsided bench there, across from some grocery store, yes, it was a sunny summery day, although it still was early spring only, and a Prince song was issuing from the open doors of that grocery, or maybe it was coming from an open window just above it, the music, it doesn't matter, Prince's hiccupping falsetto, how one didn't need to be cool to be his girl and that he knew how to undress himself, yes, and then that other, Paul Young song, all the rage at the moment, if that's the expression, constantly on the radio, about how every time you went away you took a piece of meat with you, unconscionably, in my view, yes, that's how I was hearing it then, a piece of *meat*, every time you go away you take a damn piece of meat with you, so uncool and cruel and, you know, uncalled-for, for god's sake, what's wrong with you, dump your lover if you must but leave his food alone, don't deprive him of sustenance, what the hell... yes, and how, on that visually unlovely yet sturdy and sound structurally, large bench there already was a woman, yes, I remember now, sitting on it, closer to its middle, in her thirties or forties maybe, I don't remember her well, yes, just sitting there, not reading or anything, just staring off into space, into the sunny nothing of a summery Sunday morning, perhaps daydreaming, waiting for someone to come along and start talking to her maybe, only not someone like me, that's for damn sure; and then all of a sudden I knew with total final certainty that I was dying, yes, that was it, death was sitting on that bench right next to me, invisible to everyone but me, no question about it, everything started spinning in my head and all around me, slowly at first and then with increasing acceleration, right in front of my unseeing eyes, yes, and utter despair entered my suffering soul, unconquerable weakness filled my entire being, my trembling limbs and whatnot, and I knew then that my life was over, my stupid incomplete life, and so I croaked out, hoarsely, whispered really, addressing indirectly both my bench-mate and the entire indifferent world out there, "Oh, I'm dying, I'm dying, help, please, I'm dying" (please — what, what the hell) — crushed by the realization that she, that woman on the bench, an absolute stranger, would be the last person to have ever seen me alive (and of course, I knew there was no way she could've helped me in any way, except maybe calling an emergency from the nearest phone booth, but I just needed to let at least someone, anyone, no matter who, know that those probably were going to be the last moments of my time in the world, I just had to, you know, articulate, what have you, vocalize, if that's the word, my hopeless fear and despair); and of course, upon hearing my quavering sinisterly whispering voice, that unwitting woman hastily moved further away from me on the bench, looking at me from aside with suspicion and fearful disapproval (and indeed, what a line it would be to strike up a light-hearted conversation, "I'm dying, please help" — to help one die maybe), and the next moment she just got up and walked away without looking back once, while I… well, all that matters is, I didn't die then, as I didn't die later, not so far, in too many comparable instances and on too many similar occasions to count, I'm a survivor, that's my main characteristic in life, I suppose, at which point I… and the train kept rocking and rolling, rollicking through the boundless night, and the two of us, DMD and I, were already drinking vodka, oh yes indeed, you bet, how the hell did that happen, oh no, such a surprise, inevitably, purchased by DMD from that Gorbachev-loathing yet money-loving trainwoman, and I told DMD then that I was tired, so tired, so dead-tired, man, so… about to pass out, to call it a day, call it a night, call it a life, wishing him all the best in his death, drifting off — but he told me not to… not… to… as if that was up to me, to pass out or not, with him asking me whether instead I might be willing to do him a tiny little favour, you know, help him out just a little bit, by giving him a tiny little, really minuscule push, um, in the back, in-between his shoulder blades, lovingly almost, while standing right behind him in front of the open train doors, you know, just a tiny little nudge, pretty please, lightly, lightly, ever so lightly, almost imperceptibly, unwittingly, oh would I, if he were to give that kind-hearted and equally corrupt trainwoman some serious sum of money, maybe a hundred rubles or so, half of whatever he had left on his dying persona, to incentivize her to agree opening the train door for a few moments, just a few, into the fierce howling onrush of the boundless wintry night outside, if I knew what he meant, for just one moment, for a hundred rubles or so, enough to persuade her possibly to get over her understandable worry about the possible subsequent criminal investigation into the incident, over her reluctance to be prosecuted on the grounds of harmful negligence or dereliction of duty or whatever, or maybe not, perhaps and even likely there would be nothing, no investigation, no prosecution, because who was he and what was the big deal even, sometimes a dead body in the middle of snowbound nowhere is just a dead body, sometimes it's nobody's fault, yes, so, well, would I, seriously, for real, no, seriously, and he'd give me everything he had left, the other hundred rubles from his leftover stash, and also a small handful of, like, unpolished diamonds he had there too, in a little pouch in his suitcase, seriously, don't laugh, he knew this sounded crazy, but still, might I agree, might I at least be open to the idea, yes, would I consider it, considering it would be no big deal, no big deal at all to me, just a tiny push in the back, an angelic touch, really, since I wouldn't even remember in the morning having done this, or anything, the ultimate good deed for a dying fellow-traveller, a mitzvah through and through, come to think of it, seriously… while to him, my favourite DMD, dead man dying, that would mean everything, the world, oh absolutely, and he would be grateful to me forever and ever, even in his death, and I had to agree it might be nice to have someone among the dead eternally grateful to you, a useful contact, because then, technically, it wouldn't be suicide, from, uh, whoever's powerful perspective, on the outside chance god actually existed, haha, my friend, it's complicated, because who knew, who could tell, maybe those committing suicide automatically got their chances to be reborn in the capacity of a human being diminished, if I knew what he meant, yes, maybe they, the suicide cases, got transferred to lower positions on the waiting list of planned rebirths and reincarnations, so why take chances, was he right or was he right, yes, but then on the other hand (and he raised first one of his pale vein-streaked hands off the table and then the other), why wait, what for, it probably would get ugly in the end, highly unpleasant, painful, humiliating, so why not get it over with before that starts happening, pre-emptively, proactively, in advance, right now, with a kindly accidental friend's lovely humanitarian assistance, now that he was drunk, wasted off his ass and the night was dark and the train was fast and the pristine expanse of Russian snow was freaking boundless, oh the ineffable Russian troika-balalaika, Omar Sharif and Julie Christie, and he wouldn't even feel anything at all, wouldn't know even what had happened, that one moment he was still alive, in a manner of speaking, and the next one, wham-bam, guess what, already not, so… what do you say, my friend, let's do it, huh, I beseech thee, let's just do it… and I only laughed drunkenly in response, haha, absolutely not, man, no way, you're crazy, what the hell, what the fuck, this was crazy, was he insane or something, who gave him the right to… whatever, OK, to rephrase, he had no right to take it upon himself to decide… to, uh… fucking determine if his life's ass… assignment had already been fulfilled, oh man, I was drunk and told him I wouldn't even be able to walk over there, to the train's door, plus I was no murderer, give me a break, I was leaving for America in less than two weeks and not in a million freaking years would I agree to be an accomplice to something so totally illegal and, like, unspeakable and generally totally screwed-up, even if, from his skewed perspective, I also was a dead man, to whom nothing really mattered, but metaphors be damned, I wasn't dead yet, I was not dead, no, and I wasn't dying, I… and he, nodding thoughtfully, drunkenly, mulishly, to show me he'd heard and understood me, said that was fine, if I didn't want to help him end his life, that was fine and dandy, but (or perhaps I'm just imagining this part, I don't really remember any of our exchanges beyond that point) would it be all right instead if that aforementioned sister-in-law of his were to call me sometime before my departure date, you know, so as to pass on to me something he'd written down after having been diagnosed with freaking cancer, an impromptu, accidental manuscript of sorts, in which he'd tried to recall and record everything he remembered about his freaking life, which had turned out to be surprisingly little, disappointingly and quite frighteningly so, as if most of his life had been like this train ride in the dark, with only rare and sporadic splashes of light in the distance, from Moscow to Bologoye and from Bologoye to Le… to… Le… and I said sure, why not, whatever, it wasn't going to happen anyway, she wouldn't call, so she could call, although I wouldn't be able to provide him with my freaking phone number, since I no longer had a phone at my place, nor a place of my own to have it at, either, and he didn't write any such thing, there was no manuscript, it never did happen, admit it, you dying fool — and we both laughed, and then… then nothing, I passed out, became dead to the world, and only opened my eyes to the dreary boreal darkness of a January Leningrad morning when the Red Arrow had already started to slow down in its close approaches to the Moskovsky train station, sighing and shuddering, emitting screeching metallic noises (oh, my head… my head…), and then I saw that DMD (whose real name I still remember, incidentally, but it is of no significance now… or has ever been) was not in the compartment, and neither was his old-fashioned black cardboard suitcase, as though he'd never existed in my life, never shared the drunken train ride with me, which discovery surprised and alarmed me, so much so that I went looking for the trainwoman, who was glum-looking and pointedly brusque and unpleasant, probably hungover as hell too, and who told me, in response to my halting query, with her unyielding back to me, that she had no idea where he was, that man from my compartment, and that keeping an eye on passengers' movements throughout the train was not part of her payable duties; and that reaction of hers made me convinced, somehow, that she was lying and did actually know something with regards to DMD, and for a few moments I considered pressing the issue further, perhaps with her superiors, because I was worried about him for some reason, but then… in the end, I decided against it, for I had my own life to live — which, despite my uneasy premonitions on its account at the time, still had a surprisingly long way to go before running its course.

2

TIMELESSNESS

Time wounds all heels but it doesn't heal all wounds, instead it turns the wounds into vaguely painful empty spaces within us, it makes us older, it makes us weaker, it makes us sadder and weepier, it makes us lonelier and ever more in clinging need of love, it makes us maudlin and sentimental, soft and uncertain and gullible, brittle and frail, it turns us into our real selves, the slow-walking gluttons for life's punishment... but in the end, as its sole act of kindness, it slips away quietly and leaves us alone, face to face with its eternal antagonist — timelessness.

3

EMPTINESS

Someone I've always believed to belong on the relative outskirts of my old life, a man my age, of whom I haven't had a single meaningful thought or even a momentarily heart-quickening recollection in decades, died last month, alcohol-ridden, borderline-demented and destitute, a friend who also knew him wrote to me from St. Petersburg the other day — and strangely (though not really, I suppose), I am now missing him, that seemingly and in actuality inconsequential man, distinctly if not too strongly, just wistfully and helplessly, much in the way I tend to miss my own life, in which everyone's absence, no matter how presumably immaterial, leaves a permanent and irreversible emptiness.

4

LINE IN THE SAND

After you've crossed a certain invisible line of age in the sand of time, unbeknownst to yourself, the dead become as important to you as the living, and maybe even more so, or at least, that has been the case with me, of late, as I think of them often, I hear their voices in my mind, they console and caution and comfort me, they are alive in my heart.

5

GERMANS LIKE HIM

Many — oh many — years ago, in the godawful year 1983 of our Soviet Lord Yuri Andropov, if memory serves me (it may not), back in Leningrad, in another lifetime, at an unofficial art exhibit one afternoon in a popular and also semi-clandestine basement cultural club in the heart of the heart of the city, I had a random encounter with a rather elderly and visibly inebriated man from the GDR (some may still remember that unbeautiful acronym), a fellow underground writer's acquaintance, I believe, who walked with a limp (due, as he would later cheerily volunteer, to one of his legs being shorter than the other by a few centimetres since birth) and spoke fairly good (if slightly halting and, given his condition, understandably slurred) Russian (having started studying it right after the fall of Berlin in 1945 — first on his own and then at state-run language courses… in order, presumably, to… oh, I didn't care enough to ask — to, like, maybe read Dostoyevsky in the original or whatever… just a wild guess), and he told me, in an entirely unbidden and rather inappropriately unironic revelation (but then, yet again, he was drunk), that although he had lived in Germany under Hitler and was keenly and constantly aware of the ineradicable dark stain of (granted, an absolutely ineluctable one, too, because what could one realistically do and not be disappeared on the spot, that wasn't even a question, we don't choose the times or the most essential circumstances of our lives and all that… but still, you know) mute subservience to the ugliest evil in all of documented human history which, as a result, lay forever on him and millions of other still-living Germans like him (the dead, those lucky bastards, were, of course, blessedly guilt-free), he wanted and needed (yes, needed) me to know, for some inexplicable and unwelcome reason, that every single day during those terrible interminable twelve years of Nazi rule, in the dead of night, without fail, his hand to god, in a grimly ritualistic fashion, he would write, in a feverishly hurried blind scrawl, by candlelight or in pitch-darkness (whether he'd been married, had children, what he'd been doing for a living, an accountant perhaps, an engineer, and why he hadn't been conscripted by the Wehrmacht.. ah, yes, his short leg — I wasn't curious enough to ask any of those questions), with his heart pounding away in the hollow of his ribcage, an impromptu prose poem (yes, really… if that's what it was supposed to be called) about Hitler's imminent and extremely painful death, prophesying and visualizing and describing the infernal creature's final agony in the soul-wrenching minutiae of gory details, and concluding each of those cathartic cursive eruptions with the same desperate invocation: "Die, you beastly animal, die" — and then, immediately afterwards, dizzy with momentary light-headedness, striking a match (over an ashtray, presumably, or else perhaps in the toilet) to set that little piece of notebook paper trembling in his hand on fire, liberating it from itself — and himself, from that tortured text, his sure-fire death sentence if found, every single night for all those years, yes, imagine, dear comrade — and I… suddenly and unaccountably feeling queasy with an onset of burning shame (whether it was for him or myself or all of us, I couldn't and wouldn't want to tell), filled with vague, unfocussed disgust, I only nodded silently, curtly (strike that — sympathetically), avoiding his pitiful swimming eyes, and hastened to excuse myself from his presence.

6

WALTZ No. 2

As I was walking along the crowded underpass at the downtown metro station of my destination the other Friday morning, running close to being late for my university department's monthly meeting (I don't tend to look forward to those too eagerly, if you want to know the truth), I heard, gently growing in volume and intensity, the beautiful violin rendition of Shostakovich's Waltz No. 2, accompanied somewhat less mellifluously by its regular orchestral arrangement (flutes, clarinets, saxophones, horns, trumpets, trombones... you name it), and a few seconds later I saw, seated on a red fold-out chair in a slightly slouched posture of a professional musician in the designated busking spot there, with, yes, a dully gleaming violin tucked under his jowly chin and with his protruding, heavily bagged eyes half-closed, in front of a short reedy stalk of a microphone stand and next to what appeared to be an old-school tape deck with two subwoofers, an elderly-looking man (well, he probably was my age, too, or even younger than me, it occurred to me then, in a flash of sober self-assessment, so there) possessed of an unmistakable air of being a fellow former Soviet Jew (don't ask — we just recognize each other, instantly and almost always unmistakably... thus, say, a Great Dane and a Chihuahua, upon spotting each other from a distance, know at once, in some mysterious way, that they're both dogs), and, almost despite myself, I stopped momentarily, paused in the middle of the gloomily determined and overwhelmingly young human flow, suddenly overtaken (not the right word, too overused… stirred to the deep maybe… feeling pricked in my heart... something like that) by one very specific and vivid, long-dormant recollection that had floated at that instant, out of nowhere, to the rippling surface of my mind — one of listening (and not quite listening either but being keenly aware nevertheless of its playing in the background) to this very piece of music, this ultimately nostalgic (that is to say, ineffably Russian… although, on a personal note, Putin's insane war against Ukraine has burnt all Russia-bound nostalgia out of my heart, I must say — and no great loss, good riddance) Shostakovich waltz, Waltz No. 2, in a state of quiet happiness, slowly simmering ardour, in the remote nevermore of my (did it actually happen to me, rather than someone else... yes, it did, so stop it with these rhetorical asides) youth, back in the summer or early fall of nineteen-eighty-two, I believe (the last year of Brezhnev's life, and the second one of my being automatically and forever turned down in my ill-starred application for an exit permit from the USSR), yes, a fully formed, life-like mental tableau, with me and the beautiful (yes, beautiful she was, believe me) smart funny young woman, girl that I was in love with at the time (she is dead now, as are probably, ah undoubtedly, way more than half of all the people I've ever known in my life) sitting in a beachfront restaurant, just outside of it, in Sukhumi, capital of

Abkhazia, then part of Georgia, then part of the Soviet Union, so much water under the old bridge, in another lifetime, such a different world it was then, and listening and not listening (but being immersed in and, in a manner of speaking, harmonized by it) to that waltz playing inside the restaurant, oddly enough, and reaching us, instead of the ubiquitously hellacious early-eighties potpourri of Pugacheva-Rotaru-Kobzon-Leontyev-Senchina-Khil'-Obodzinsky and… so on, and it was, of course, inexpressibly good (forgive me, for I know not how else to put it), all of it, just being there and, you know, existing, being existed, as Thomas Bernhard put it in *The Loser*, being alive (yes, I know, this is overwritten — but what can I do) and listening to it, that beautiful otherworldly waltz, just the two of us, the only two people there, late at night, well past midnight, drinking cold semi-sweet Psou, the local wine taking its name from the river separating Abkhazia from Russia, as we had been told by our waiter, and (yes, that's right, true fact) I was reciting to her the entirety of Arseny Tarkovsky's long poem "Life, Life," the one claiming that there is no death in the world, no death, with everyone and everything being immortal, the one he recited himself off-screen in his son's film *Mirror* (which I'd loved, if that's the right word for it, and she hadn't seen), "I don't believe in premonitions / and omens frighten me not," yes, all that, and we were young and the world was endless and full of infinity and immortality, while the dark waves of the eternal Black Sea, unseen in the dark, were lapping on the pebbly shore, rhythmically, methodically, ceaselessly, thousands millions trillions of them, sibilant, whooshing and susurrating in the pitch-darkness surrounding the narrow circle of yellow light from the restaurant in which we were bathed in night's fragrant warmth, to put it maybe a bit too beautifully, and that Shostakovich waltz was still playing, in that another life, the long-gone one, all these compressed multicoloured layers of petrified decades ago… and for an instant, already back in the present moment of my being, back in that metro underpass, in my current reality (in which Russia was a fascist state waging an unconscionable war against Ukraine, the American political system was broken and dysfunctional, a dozen eggs at my local supermarket cost over 6 Canadian dollars, and I was almost late for my department meeting), an old (OK, let me be kind to myself and say — middle-aged) man, former Soviet Jew, stopping momentarily in the long underpass at a busy downtown metro station in order to listen to an almost certainly another middle-aged former Soviet Jew play Shostakovich's Waltz No. 2 on his violin, and yes, I also wondered briefly, gripped by the music's mnemonic power over me (and not for the first time, of late) why my memories of my first life, so to speak (yes, so to speak — it is a pretentious way to put it, I know, but what does it matter if that's how I feel about my so-called life… and besides, I'm entitled to my own tacky verbal tics, am I not), the one that had begun at the same starting point for everyone who's ever been born and ended when, at thirty, I boarded that silvery shark of a West-bound plane at Leningrad's Pulkovo airport — why, in short, my memories of it, my first life (yes, I know, but kindly just let it go), were quite so much stronger, more vibrant, intense and keenly and sharply detailed and delineated than those of, well, pretty much everything (no, not everything, come on) that came later, but this was a pointless and counterproductive line of contemplation, a waste of rapidly dwindling time, under the circumstances, and so I thought instead that he (the said sad violinist in front of me) definitely reminded me of someone, and someone really good and kind, at that, and... yes, of course, I realized, he reminded me of the great Soviet chess player from Leningrad, Victor Korchnoi, that's who, a chess genius, who almost succeeded at beating in a crazily tumultuous match for the world championship the official Soviet paragon of sports patriotism and Komsomol goody-two-shoes, slick-haired and reedy-voiced Anatoly Karpov, in Baguio, in the Philippines, in nineteen-seventy-eight, a few years following his (Korchnoi's) defection from the Soviet Union and thus automatically becoming a contemptible, death-deserving traitor to the Motherland in the bovine eyes of the official Soviet propaganda, which last fact caused every decent and even minimally enlightened Soviet person at the time to root for him with added passion, to say nothing about the insignificant little me, a young and idealistic (strike that) Leningrad Jew, with his perennially inflamed imagination, to whom he (Korchnoi) always reminded of his own father, my father, in some powerful and poignant yet elusive fashion, in the way he talked, by the cadences of his speech, the timbre of his voice, in the little gesticular (probably not a real word, but oh well, them's the breaks) quirks and mannerisms of his (he was even born the same year as my father... two remarkably bright and good Leningrad Jews, two mensches, I always wanted to be like them, but...), but that too unfortunately was an extraneous and superfluous thought at that specific moment, and I mentally shook my head and my whole inner self, like a dog coming out of water, only inwardly, to awaken myself fully to the unkind reality of my and our now (in which I was inexorably getting old and running late for my department meeting), and took a quick step, half-step toward the still-playing (but already winding down that unforgettable waltz of my youth) violinist, in order to give him some money and, you know, say something nice and comforting to him maybe, in Russian (like what, though — that death doesn't exist, as per the poet Arseny Tarkovsky... that life is something to be endured and there is no shame in succumbing to its relentless toughness, so take heart, my dear man... that we, the adult-age first-generation immigrants from a totalitarian world, were supposed and indeed fully expected by life and, well, Mother Nature itself maybe to be the lost cause of our own desperate endeavors from the get-go, in terms of our inevitable constant heartbreaks and readily predictable setbacks and our glaring non-achievements, yes, us, the loveable and pitiable losers at life by default, whether beautiful or not, in our fellow Montrealer Leonard Cohen's florid poetic assignation, but losers all the same... oh man, what's this life of ours, what has it done to us, just look at us, how old we are all of a sudden, this is just sad, life, life, but at least, at the very least you're a brilliant violinist, yes, which is nothing to sneeze at, if probably a little too old by now to be hired by a real symphony orchestra or some such outfit, if you want the hard truth of it, not that you don't know it already, but that's life, it's cruel and cold and it doesn't care about us or anyone, but it's essential for us to believe that we haven't lived completely in vain, no, not completely, oh man, not totally, and as for me, well, I may seem to be doing moderately all right from the outside, holding it together, as they say, on the surface of my middle-class existence and all that, but I'll have you know that I also happen to be a walking compendium, if that's the word, of regrets and unrealized dreams, which is not healthy from any standpoint, to put it mildly, so… and yet, and yet… man, we should take succor — if that's the word, succor, solace, no matter — in the knowledge that our children, let alone grandchildren, if or when we do have them, will be and already are the legitimate, true-blue, perfectly free citizens of the free world, regardless of how terminally screwed up it appears to be at this juncture, with their lives turning out to be infinitely better and more successful than ours, and that's the principle upon which the world pivots, if that's the way to put it, and so on, and… well, something like that maybe, some such platitudes I could impart to him, just to make him feel better or something, ridiculous, of course, and presumptuous, he was stranger of whom I knew nothing… but oh well), but just as I made to approach him, I realized, much to my embarrassed frustration and dismay, that I had no money to give him, none, because I had no cash on me, nothing in my pockets or in my wallet, zero cash situation (and I noticed, too, that hardly anyone thus far had dropped any loonies or toonies, much less any paper money into the beat-up violin case unfolded, agape, at his splayed, shoddily shod feet… and actually, I thought, it'd been quite a while since I had any actual, real money on my persona, unless I was travelling abroad... because why would I or anyone do this anymore, carry any physical money, when we had our multiplicity of cards and smartphones... cash was becoming obsolete, extinct, already practically out the door, OK, and so, how — but again, this was another mental distraction, my mind was all over the place — were they supposed to survive now, going forward, all those cash-incentivized metro musicians and street buskers everywhere... they could not, it wasn't even a question), and for a split second I was considering making a mad dash for the nearest ATM outlet, the one just outside the metro station, half a block away, even less than that maybe, next door to my university building, yes, but that, of course, would mean taking the escalator upstairs, leaving the station, running over to the ATM in question (and hoping there would be no line inside its airless cubicle), procuring the money (but then, too, the smallest denomination I would obtain from it would be a $20 bill — so then, would I give him that, of course not, that would be too damn ostentatious and tacky, like I was some kind of freaking Abramovich), then rushing back and re-entering the metro, getting on the down escalator, and... well, in other words, that was out of the question, obviously, since I was already officially late for the department meeting (although, in all frankness, nothing of any import were to happen if I showed up for it as much as an hour late, or even skipped it altogether, but... since I'd already left my house on a snowy Friday morning, reluctantly, and made my joyless way downtown, what would be the point of having done it in vain, effectively for nothing — so self-defeating), and so, with an appropriately contrite look on my face (and I was feeling bad about this, for real), I stepped up closer to him, just as he was getting being done with the waltz's final chords, and said to him, quickly and quietly, in Russian, "Thank you, and I mean it, you play very beautifully, man, this brought back some lovely memories from my youth, but unfortunately, I have no money on me, see, I'm embarrassed to say… but next time, if you ever play in this spot again, I promise to make it up to you" — and my heart was beating rapidly in my chest for no clear reason — and (life, life) he just looked at me in mild confusion, lifting up at me those moist, heavily bagged soulful eyes of his, those of a violin-playing human basset hound, and smiled thinly and shrugged apologetically, and responded, in perfectly neutral American-Canadian English, "Sorry, my friend, I don't understand" — oh, son of a gun (life, life)… and, feeling like an idiot (you could say that again), like a stranger to myself, I just repeated the same (not quite the same, of course) in English, what I'd just said to him in Russian, only less empathically, with less of an emotional acceleration (and he inclined his head politely and said, in a voice slightly hoarse from a spell of non-use, "Thank you kindly, I appreciate it, and no problem, I understand, this happens all the time") — and then, no longer feeling or thinking about anything in particular (not even the department meeting, already in progress… this happens all the time), I turned away from him and hurried towards the up escalator.

7

OTHER PEOPLE

Most of our thoughts are memories, most of our memories are imaginary, most of what we are is other people.

8

AFTERLIFE WI-FI

He told her not to be too heartbroken, this was not the end, because there was bound to be some kind of wi-fi in the afterlife, so she would hear from him as soon as he got there, went through whatever registration procedure was necessary for the new arrivals, probably changed into some kind of afterlife clothes, oriented himself a bit in spaceless timelessness, and then she could expect to hear from him, he really believed that, speaking both metaphorically and not, cross my heart, no need to cry, my love.

9

PEN MAN SHIP

If I close my eyes now (even if while still keeping them open, if that makes any sense to you... as it does to me), with surprisingly little effort, it seems, I can become again a seven-year-old boy a lifetime ago (OK, let's try to say something a bit more interesting and less repetitive than that), in another lifetime (OK, well...), sitting in a tall chair (what kind of chair, specifically, describe it... no, don't feel like it) at a round dinner table of old and tired dark wood next to my father (he's a promising young scientist in the super-duper-secret field of, you know, submarine electromagnetism, and what I do not know yet, as a seven-year-old — and wouldn't find out for a whole lot more years — is that when graduating from high school, he had wanted and hoped to become a doctor, but back at the time, in late forties-early fifties, in the fetid political atmosphere of late-Stalinist anti-Semitism and so on quickly building up to the so-called Doctor's Plot, which... well, those who don't know what it was could easily google it... anyway, in those years, young people with the word Jew written on the infamous fifth line of their internal Soviet passports were strongly and officially discouraged from entering the medical profession, so... and incidentally, at seven, I don't know yet that we're Jews, which is an unlucky lottery ticket in the Soviet

Union or, broader, Russia, I would only be informed about that little detail of my being, by my parents, in a serious sit-down talk, sometime the following year, and that would be such a heart-stopping shock to the little me, such... oh god, we — me included — were those horrible, incorrigible, evil people I'd heard so much about from boys and older women down in the courtyard, it was us, me, oh no...), underneath an intensely and comfortingly (well, how else would I put it) harsh, yellow-shaded lightbulb suspended from the murky concave ceiling on a twisted length of black cord, in our oddly-shaped single room with a humming wall-to-wall woodstove (on whose endlessly repeated pattern of pale-blue ceramic tiles, the abnormally, Uncle Styopa the Militiaman-tall — yes, sure, do google Uncle Styopa, or not, if you so wish, because what does it ultimately matter; google on the name Sergei Mikhalkov... Mikhalkov, indeed, quite the family — Tsar Peter, the Dutch shipbuilder, the mad, both literally and metaphorically, founder of this astounding, geographically accursed city of our lives, Leningrad, is depicted, striding purposefully along with a clay smoking pipe in his resolutely clenched... um, jaw... mouth) and the hopelessly and sadly discordant Red October piano in the corner (in the corner of an oval-shaped room, huh... well, OK, whatever, moving right along), in a large (make it mid-sized) communal apartment (in a nutshell — doors to rooms on both sides of a long, very long dark corridor, sinuous, snake-like, the terrible dead, bone-dry river whose ominously towering banks... too many adverbs... cliffs, like... think Grand Canyon, well, no, not quite, not at all... over decades have been papered with consecutive layers of frayed newsprint, turned yellow in the dry water of time, all that insanely cruel and actually just insane Soviet history, Lord almighty, of which neither I nor other kids living in the apartment are aware of in the slightest, obviously, blissfully happy, running up and down that corridor of horror, yes, OK, and then one thoroughly unusable bathroom, at corridor's end, where in the indescribable bathtub occupied by a pair of ancient Army boots, not a joy to behold, and an exceptionally ugly-looking oaken barrel of no longer edible pickled mushrooms, fairly bursting up on itself, amid the overpowering yet also endearingly familiar and nostalgia-generating and soothing reek of chlorine, one toilet next to the bathroom, with lines of people forming in front of it along the corridor first thing in the morning and, well, last thing in the evening, and on the left, one — well, sure — kitchen, with an unclothed rickety table in the middle, and one gas stove with four burners... no refrigerator, that's right, absolutely none — not sure how to translate *antresoli*, other than maybe ceiling closet space in the corridor, you get the point and the picture) in the roiling heart (roiling, huh, what an odd adjective... knock it off, if possible — all this... writing) of Dostoyevsky's Petersburg (whether I would have heard that odd reference on the radio, as a child, at the time when Dostoyevsky's very name, not to mention his books, deemed full of bourgeois individualism under Stalin, had only been unbanned but a few years earlier, with the onset of what would come to be commonly known by the historians of the era as the Khrushchevian thaw, I cannot be sure; and of course, the very sound of the name Petersburg, the great city's pre-Great October Socialist Revolution, tzarist-era moniker, evokes nothing but strictly bad and loathsome connotations in my young mind, but… but what… OK, yes, but regardless, without quite knowing how I know it, I do know what this inexpressible city of mine is, what it is to me — grey stone and Karelian granite, the Swiss cheese of its interconnecting inner courtyards, the silvery mercury of the heavy water in the Neva, the occasional and always surprising ringing silences of transparently sun-filled cobwebbed early-autumn street corners in our part of it, amid the ceaseless hustle and bustle and whatnot of the heart of the heart of the… OK, moving on… and the massive old and indeed totally Dostoyevskean apartment tenements, no matter who that fellow Dostoyevsky may have been, and… and the long-accustomed-to stench from the nearby Obvodny Canal, the city's main open-air sewage artery, with its frighteningly stagnant, dead water, and, uh… let me think, I can't quite re-inhabit my long-nonexistent seven-year-old self right on the spot, on such a short notice, can I… yes, and the simmering dusky milky light of mosquito-ridden summer nights, no more mentioning Dostoyevsky, I promise, I don't like him as a writer to begin with, and the unconquerable triumphant limitless darkness of the city's boreal winters, how I miss it, seriously, and… well, the swarm of human masses in front of the aforesaid Varshavsky and Baltiisky train stations just across the hump-backed bridge over the Obvodny, and… oh, and the little life-sized Lenin, looking coy and, wouldn't you know it, loveable, totally not inaccessible, sacrilegious as that may sound, in a shallow niche in train station's wall, and the brand-new, ultra-modern Frunzensky Department Store, the second-largest in the city, maybe even in the country, well, no, that we're all so understandably proud of, and… and of course, the Soviet Navy ships on the Neva that my father took me to look at one day back at the end of July, those grey whales, and that little ship on top of the Admiralty's spire, the symbol of the city, and… and so infinitely, endlessly, impossibly much more; the more I, a seven year-old boy in the evening, keep thinking about it all, me and my city and… all the rest of it, there is way more to think about, of course, and it's just too much for me, too much world, and the more I remember the more there is to remember still, as memories seem to come in the process of remembering, an infinity of them, flowing unto goddamn eternity, except that… well, our mortal lives are anything but eternal… no, wait, I don't know that yet, at seven I'm immortal); and… well, and… and all of the above notwithstanding, or getting past it, and thinking and not thinking at once about everything and nothing, I'm writing out, with a nobly gleaming (strike that, what exactly is gleaming and why it is doing so nobly — that's just writing) yellow wooden dip pen, *ruchka-vstavochka* (and a half-empty ink pot is just a few centimetres away and to the right of me on the table, by father's unyielding elbow, as well as a stack of soft and fluffy pink squares of blotting paper), in a standard faded-green elementary-school notebook with eight lined pages, all the thirty-three (by the number of teeth in a grown human being's mouth, it occurs to me, and I can't help chuckling to myself… no, not really, that's a fib, if that's the right word, that's not the seven-year-old me, it's my present-moment's self, the one of the quiet twilight of my life) letters of the Russian alphabet, slowly, time and again, practising my, umm, penmanship, oh screw that (but no, I'm a good boy, and I always listen to and obey the grown-ups, especially my father) as per our first-grade teacher's assignment (Kira Sergeyevna, her name was, that I remember, while having forgotten, somehow, much of everything else about my life), improving my inchoate handwriting, first the capitals and then the lowercase ones, the tip of my tongue sticking out, **Aa** (America is the historically doomed citadel of the international imperialism, America is the land of yesterday, world of the past, lagging behind us forever, Americans are eternally sad and miserable because they're being exploited by their, uh, exploiters and, like, the Pentagon, Americans are deeply and hopelessly envious of us, the Soviet people, for a host of obvious reasons, and our hearts do go out to them, but within the bounds of reason, because there is such a thing as one's personal responsibility for the... OK, they should know what I mean, those Americans, and the bottom line is, they all just need to rise up against their ruling class of capitalist bloodsuckers and shadowy billionaires and have themselves a proletarian revolution and, you know, join us in our purposeful march towards our radiant communist future... and granted, I've never seen a single real live American in my life, in all of my seven years on earth, except on television, and yes, we do have a TV-set, OK, later, later, don't get distracted, where they look like more or less normal people, those Americans, only sad and miserable, although of course they are different from us, they must be... those poor sad Americans... and yes, like I just said, or thought, we do have a TV-set, our family does, the only one in the entire communal apartment, it's tiny — the TV-set, not the apartment — and comes with a set of, like, two conjoined convex lenses of thick glass, a funhouse aquarium of sorts, which gets filled with tap water and then attached to the front of the palm-sized TV-screen for magnifying purposes), **Бб** (my little brother's first name starts with this letter, but also… the beautifully voiceless… as I've heard him being described by someone, I don't remember who, probably my grandmother, the Leningrad one, Mark Bernes, grandfather's favourite singer, who sings about thinking of his love on a dark, dark night during the Great Patriotic War, and I only have one grandfather, he and my other grandmother live in a lovely quiet suburb of Moscow, called Moose Island, and I had lived with them there for a year, just two long years ago, he's a Party representative at a large tire-making factory and she is a school principal and teacher of biology and Soviet anatomy, but OK, no getting distracted again, and also Mark Bernes sings about how much he loves life, every Sunday morning or maybe even more frequently, and also about the fact that the Russian people, as such, such as they are, of all the people in the world, don't want war, and he also is a Jew, but I don't know that yet either… not that it matters, OK, so stop bringing it up all the time, the point's already been made, although it's not clear what it was… and, well, it actually mattered — a lot, an awful lot — in the old Soviet Union, whether one was Jewish or not… oh really, you don't say, Captain Obvious), and also Agniya Barto, one of my most favourite children's poets, "Anna-Vanna, our Young Pioneers' detachment would like to see the piglets," **Вв** (by the way, apparently,

Leonardo da Vinci was half-Jewish too, as it has just been discovered, like Hemingway when he was a child, it's a childish Soviet rhyme — stop blabbering, stop getting distracted all the time, what's wrong with you, what the hell are you even talking about — I mean, now, sixty years later, it was discovered somehow that his mother was Jewish, huh… sun of a gun… it's a pun), **Гг** (my mother's first name starts with this letter, so I love it, and of course, it is the first letter of Yuri Gagarin's last name, while also being the first letter of the first name of Gherman Titov, the Soviet cosmonaut number two — his appearance probably was a bit less iconically, emblematically, quintessentially Russian than Gagarin's, smile less multi-dimpled, personality a bit less gregarious, so that's why, I suppose…), **Дд** (it's evening, I feel warm, starting to doze off, and coming from far away, it seems, my father's voice is stern, though not angry, as he reminds me that penmanship is important and that… and he's saying that, oh he's telling me that, you know, *The New Yorker* magazine would only accept a story if it was neatly written out by hand, it's a well-known fact, although of course neither one of us has ever heard of any such magazine, it goes without saying, to which I retort by pointing out to him that the magazine in question wouldn't accept a story consisting of just one scene, regardless of the quality of its writing, much less the quality of its author's penmanship… all the more so that what we have here so far, dad, is not even a scene but rather an extended and fairly incoherent exposition, so… but on the other hand, who sez exposition is not a scene and a scene not a story and why cannot a story consist of nothing but writing, and… and he nudges me in the elbow with his elbow), **Ee** (Evgeny Evtushenko is still young but already one of the Soviet Union's most famous and internationally renowned poets, and it was him who wrote that song they play on the radio all the time, about how Russians don't want war; his real last name is Gangnus, it's German, which is neither here nor there, and I wouldn't learn that pointless factoid until decades later also, or either, like so many other things in my life, Mark Bernes sings it, that song, voicelessly and beautifully, as I already said, or maybe not, and…), **Ёё** (with all those songs, with all those cosmonauts, with… with all that great literature, all that art, all that ballet, all those… all that… well, just look at Russia now, o Lord, just look at it and shudder with sorrow and disgust, and… just smite it already or something), **Жж** (almost every morning back then began with Mark Bernes's singing on the radio, both in the kitchen and in our room, about his being in love with life, that he loved it anew again and again, which, he admitted in the same song, was nothing new, of course, but still, still… it was good to know, that he loved life so much… damn liar), **Зз** (America was historically doomed, the world of imperialism was historically doomed, the West was historically doomed, the collective West was America — the epicentre and root cause of all the evil in the world, so there), **Ии** (our family name starts with this letter, enough said), **Кк** (this is probably autumn, fall, there is fire going on, cheerily and cozily, in our Tsar-Peter woodstove, November maybe, no, October, more likely, and so by this point I've already been told that come next summer — a lifetime away, to be sure, for a seven-year-old, but still, you know, within the realm of the imaginable — we will be moving out of our single room in this communal apartment and, much to my parents' extreme and almost obscene excitement, getting to occupy a separate cooperative, or whatever it's called, three-room apartment of our own on the outskirts of the city, in what could be another world, somewhere on an as-yet-nonexistent Cosmonauts Avenue, which… no, I can't be thinking about this now, it's too sad and horrible, it's going to be the end of my world as it's known to me, the end, it's… but no, I can't and won't be thinking about that now, I forbid myself), **Лл** (Larissa is the name of the girl from my first-grade class that I like, and the thought of never seeing her again, because that Cosmonauts Avenue could just as well be located in the Soviet Far East, eleven time zones away, as far as I am concerned, since Leningrad is so enormous and I am so small and, you know, like, totally devoid of any mobile geographic autonomy, well, that thought is just breaking my little heart, and I forbid myself, I forbid, **Мм** (my first name starts with this letter, and that's important, because I am important, I am very important to the world, for the world only exists for as long as I exist in it… no, wait, that doesn't sound right… well, yes, it does, and I also am eternal and immortal)… and so on, writing them out, those letters, with much care and deliberation, cautiously, timidly, all across the page's expanse, **Хх** (the most popular dirty word in all of the Russian language, the greatest language in the world, as everyone in the world knows and acknowledges, starts with this letter, that word, yes, and I'm not supposed to know it, let alone ever say it, not even in my head, and… well, I don't believe my mother or either one of my two grandmothers, say, ever uttered it in their entire lives, but... well, how can one not know it, even at my age, when everyone down in the courtyard and out in the streets says it all the time, all the men and boys and even some women, and even some people in our communal apartment, too, and it is stenciled everywhere crudely in dirty chalk or with a lump of coal, on every wall of every other building in our part of the city, it seems, that simple and catchy three-letter word, including the dark dank walls of the archway that leads from the cavern of our inner courtyard to the street and the larger outside world, and... I can't help half-giggling, while writing out this letter, and my father notices, of course, and he shakes his head disapprovingly, telling me again to concentrate, because penmanship is important), **Цц** ("chicken fried, chicken steamed went out to walk along the Nevsky," I start murmuring inwardly or maybe just very softly under my breath that silly old street or folk or something like that song that everyone knows but no one knows where or why they know it, "it was caught, it was arrested, it was told to show its passport" — and my father starts humming it too involuntarily, smiling, in my imagination), **Чч** (Charlie Chaplin, Korney Chukovsky, the idols of my chi... but no, no, I cannot do this, this is just too much for me, I can't, because once you've started, where do you stop, I'm unstoppable, my train of thought is, my river of memory, for I've already had seven years' worth of an eternity of words and names and... and memories, yes, and thoughts and... and now it's many decades later, it's evening, it's dark outside...), **Шш Щщ** (silence, silence), **Ээ** (eternity, eh... well, OK, no problem, I'll rein myself in), **Юю** (my father's name starts with this letter, so it's time to calm down, no one is dying yet, far from it, and all is good with the world), and fnally, **Яя** (and that's me, I, the last letter of the alphabet, as every single Russian-speaking child will have heard countless times from his or her kindergarten or elementary-school teacher… yes, me, whom everyone loves and who will never die — the last letter of the alphabet), and yes, writing those letters out under my father's watchful gaze, as if he had nothing better to do with his precious time this evening, and listening to him instruct me to do it again, again, and again (fail better, fail better, better fail, better fail better, sure, Beckett, sure, thanks a bunch), patiently, painstakingly, diligently, gradually and inexorably bettering myself, because penmanship (I know, it's a stupid-sounding word, but it's the only one I have for you, because quarrelling with or about words is a waste of time, and in Russian penmanship is *chistopisaniye*, literally clean writing, incidentally, and… penmanship, pen-man-ship, pen man ship, man with a pen on a ship — this sounds like that cognitive test Trump kept crowing about non-stop a while back, unforgettably enough, right — person woman man camera TV… god) is important not as such, per se (per se, per se, whatever), but as a tool, so to speak, for developing your character, your concentration, your attention to detail, your inner fastidiousness (say what… I don't understand… my head is swimming) and dignity of spirit (all those words) and… while my mother and our (my brother's and mine) live-in nanny Lyuba (a poorly educated peasant girl, now — inconceivably — already almost close to or past the age of twenty, which of course is really old, originally from the Volga-bound city of Cheboksary, capital of the Chuvash Autonomous

Soviet Socialist Republic, who's been living with us without an official city permit since I came into the world, in some unclear manner or another, having been dropped by some random wayward crane from the sky and right into our room in our communal apartment, some such stuff, such nonsense, and who secretly and unbelievably believes in God, which could turn out to be a seriously dangerous circumstance for her, were that shameful secret of hers to come out… somehow, had I been a worse person than I am, had I not loved her so much, had I not… well, but never in a million years would I as much as consider ratting her out, if that's the expression, and who has a painted paper portrait of some woman distantly resembling my mother whom she, Lyuba, probably my favourite person in the whole world, claims ridiculously to be God's mother, and she keeps that painting rolled-up and all hidden among her tangled clothing items in the black cardboard suitcase with her scant earthly possessions, as she calls her… well, her earthly possessions) are in the communal kitchen, my mother and Lyuba are, where the rest of the women of the apartment also have congregated in significant numbers, probably, definitely, each one waiting for her turn to wash the dishes or something like that before going back inside their rooms to their families, or the absence thereof, and preparing to turn in for the night or… yes, there, in the kitchen, where the radio, that black felt dish on the wall, is droning on, by turns ominously and, like, ecstatically, maybe and probably at some point on the subject of Cuba ("Cuba, my love" — I sing this fiercely beautiful, blood-stirring song all the time, accompanying myself on our sadly inadequate Red October piano with one finger), and how Cuba is an island of crimson dawns and anti-imperialist freedom and unvanquishable peace and forever-irreversible socialism-communism, if you know what I mean, and how the currently ongoing or still very recent so-called Caribbean Crisis (OK, so we're in October still then, or early November at the latest) has been created by the very unattractively dying and still deadly dangerous in its agony poisonous snake of American imperialism, otherwise known as the Pentagon, and then the beautifully voiceless Mark Bernes, my grandfather's favourite (you already said that, so... enough), starts singing about how if you want to know whether Russian people want war you should ask that question of the silence over the infinite expanse of Russia's fields of grain and her grasslands (already said that, too, if not in so many words... clean writing, clean writing), as well as the Russian soldiers that are in the ground in eternal sleep, under the Russian birch trees, in silence eternal, and... and my little brother, OK, where is he, by the way, speaking of silence (the main source of which in our room and in the apartment writ large he never happens to be, if you know what I mean), well, yes, he must be with my grandmother, the Leningrad one, my father's mother, who lives with the rest of her extended family, which is our family too, obviously (all of them are dead now, just saying, with one exception, unbelievably.... well, believe it), consisting, in addition to her and her mother (my great-grandmother, who is extremely old indeed and used to be married before the Revolution to a wealthy merchant or someone like that, and because of his wealth both of them had been permitted to live in Petersburg, despite the fact that Jews normally were not permi,.. but OK, come on, I don't know yet, at seven years of age, anything about our being Jewish, as it has been made abundantly clear more than once here, so don't even go there, stop getting distracted, carried away)… so, that extended family, that of her (grandmother's) older brother, an important figure in the Soviet cellulose industry, and his English-teaching wife and their three sons, my uncles, all three full of fun and vim (vim? zest? piss and vinegar? come on) and great and positive energy and, like, mischief and jollity and… mathematical ability, too, it should be mentioned (although why), my father's age and younger; plus they have a permanent housekeeper, living with them, practically a member of the family, an older relative of Lyuba's, her aunt, also from Cheboksary, yes, that's the connection, always so friendly and sweet, over on Sixth Red Cavalry Street, in an almost unprecedentedly large rambling (my parents describe it as such) single-family (no one else but them lives there) apartment with a perfectly tuned concert piano (in a whole different class from our sad old Red October) and a special library room, where no one lives, nothing but books there and a plush blue couch, with some of those books in English, the willy-nilly chosen language of international imperialism, yes, actually published abroad, those books, in actual capitalist England, having been held in their foreign hands by real actual foreigners, pretty incredible (one such old book there, about the jollity of jolly good England, with photographs from the beginning of the century, was one of my favourites, decades later, it would come into my possession, and then I would take it with me to America, that's how much I loved it, and then it would end up being lost there, in America, already in the nineties, along with sundry other memorabilia, in the only one of the twenty-six boxes FedExed by me from Minneapolis to a friend's house in New York City that never arrived to its destination, but… well, no, I'm not getting into that now, all those losses, losses, way too many layers of life to be dealt with, life, life….), plus, of course, the Great Soviet Encyclopaedia, those fifty-two dark-blue volumes filled with facts and factual lies and shameless propaganda (but I don't know that yet, do I, that it's mostly lies and propaganda, and I'm just fascinated by it, all that knowledge, all that infinity of information, as I would remain through the rest of my life, such as it has turned out to be, forever immersed in encyclopedias and dictionaries and… well, OK, some other time), just an unhurried few-minute walk from us, that apartment was, or to quote the famous Bee Gees song, "…you can tell by the way I use my walk I'm a woman's man, no time to talk" (what the hell was that, where did it come from… get a grip), and where the… OK, concentrate, concentrate, what the hell, you're not making sense… (**Аа Бб Вв Гг Дд**… and well, I used to write everything by hand, pretty much, all my so-called literary, samizdat texts, such as they were, always the first draft would be in longhand, and probably the second one also, and only then, afterwards, later would I go on the typewriter, four layers max of black rustling nasty finger-smudging copying paper, my clanky-clunky old metallic German typewriter, all those underground texts, mine and those of other people, typing and retyping, endlessly, banging away with two fingers, lifelong habit since those days, current students of mine still occasionally ask me why I'm banging away on my laptop, as if it were my enemy, still with two, maybe three, four fingers tops, well, I'm not a blind typist, as per the Russian expression, can you type blindly, they would ask, and no, I'm not a blind typist, nowhere near, and nor am I bilingual, incidentally, not even close, no, I'm a native speaker of Russian who knows English well and is capable of writing Russian sentences in English, if you know what I mean, which you probably don't, because I wouldn't be able to explain it myself, even to myself)… and yes, that's right, says the radio (I don't need to hear it to know what it's saying, almost at any given moment, and it's always on, down in the kitchen), comrade Fidel's Cuba, he and his barbudos, with our indispensable help, will absolutely defeat evil America, once and for all, and the historically doomed world of imperialism should make no mistake on the subject of its being historically doomed, it is playing with fire, isn't it, which it shouldn't be doing, because we're a nuclear superpower, which is nothing to sneeze at, while it's so cozily dark and warmly cold outside, in that velveteen darkness, October, October, early November, in the heart of Leningrad, oh my love, my glorious city, why art thou Leningrad, which I haven't really seen all that much of yet, by the by, in my seven years in this world, on this earth, but so what, I have time to see it still, to learn every one of its hidden secrets, its nooks and multitudinous crannies, nothing but time, my love, my life is endless, even if now it's drawing inexorably to a close, OK, good, no problem, and here in this oval-shaped room we have our fire, our friendly anti-imperialist Soviet fire going on in our Tsar-Peter ceramic woodstove, so I can be working on my freaking pen-man-ship in perfect comfort, indeed in a state of quiet happiness, bliss, a little soporifically maybe, for it's getting late (but dad, there still is no story here, in all of this, not even a single-scene one, see, just a lot of damn exposition, dad, it's not a story, not a story still... well, maybe later, maybe, at some point it will emerge, someplace else — and incidentally, on a brighter note, all through my school years, teachers have always praised my handwriting, my penmanship, my clean writing, and on one occasion, even a KGB kulturtraeger, if that's a word, a censor from the organs, had praised it, too, saying that it gave him pleasure on a purely aesthetic level to look at handwritten drafts of my as-yet-untyped stories and, like, essays and stuff in samizdat manuscripts, which he couldn't say the same of my fellow underground-writer anti-Soviet element, wouldn't you know it, how nice; but now my handwriting is all but gone, rendered unneeded by decades of unuse, oh well...), and I'm thinking of how damn lucky I am, oh I know, I know, all of us are, to be living in Leningrad, that unrepeatable city, our country's cultural capital, in the future-bound Soviet Union, how did I even get so insanely lucky, to have had that figurative crane drop me into my parents' metaphoric cabbage patch in the heart of Leningrad, USSR, instead of America, for instance — the terrible world of humankind's ugly past and capitalist exploitation of the ordinary proletarians like us, yes, what a disaster that would have been (and yes, although I am a middle-class former Soviet Jewish Canadian-American and vice-versa, I don't exploit anyone, I am not a capitalist, I am not an imperialist, I'm just trying to help young North American students of creative writing to become, well, better writers, although I cannot really help myself in that respect, but that's just the way it goes… pen man ship, clean writing, clean writing), while my father, dead for a quarter of a century now, whom I've already outlived, is telling me again not to get distracted, to concentrate on my penmanship, because he can see I'm thinking of something… extraneous, of what, of… what has happened to us all, us and our former god-accursed Motherland, of the horror and pure unmitigated evil that Russia has become now, my or anyone else's penmanship notwithstanding, but now is not the time, concentrate, concentrate, exist in the moment, shut out all the distractions, he is telling me, know that everything in your life worth paying attention to is right here and now, right here and right now, right in front of and around you, as it always has been, always will be, here and now, and nothing else matters, nothing else has even begun to exist yet, only these letters emerging from under your pen, **Аа Бб Вв Гг Дд Ее Жж Зз… Зз… ззззз…** letters letters letters and sentences… pen man ship pen man ship clean writing clean writing…

10

ROAD LONG

One man wrote one hundred thousand words about the road unfolding before him, but then, in an onset of mental rigorousness, having decided that one hundred thousand words was perhaps a little too many, he commenced to edit the text with severe determination, crossing out one passage after another, getting rid of whole disjointed legions' worth of adverbs and adjectives, keen as a hawk on leaving in only the most essential information about his journey, until finally, already at the end of his life, what he was left with was, simply, just two words: "Road Long."

11

FIRST AND LAST

People are always asked about their first childhood memory — the first one they were able to put in words as adults — but never about their last one — the first and the last they would never share with anyone, themselves included.

12

UNIMAGINABLE

Imaginable is real, we know as much, but unimaginable is even more so, since most people end up living the lives they could not have predicted for themselves when they were little.

13

MAY12: THE WOLF

After the film about the unspeakably contemptible, although masquerading as an ordinary normal Soviet patriot, and eventually inevitably unmasked closer to the end by the ever-unerring and never-dormant steely-eyed and ruthlessly kind-hearted organs and justly punished by the latter to the ultimate degree of our merciless proletarian justice already beyond the darkening silver screen, traitor to the Motherland, incomprehensibly an absolutely seemingly ordinary normal Motherland-loving and Fatherland-abiding Soviet citizen by the looks of him, nothing outwardly unusual about his countenance and what in the world had to have happened to him so... so... unspeakable that he became a traitor working for money for the infernal citadel of international imperialism, how in hell (strike that) that could possibly come about, how did his inner traitor grow inside him unnoticedly to those around him, like a poisonous mushroom, no, a tumour, yes, a human-sized deadly tumour the size of a poisonous mushroom, only a lot larger, and then all of a sudden it was already too late for him, as that inner traitor of his just up and swallowed him whole from within and in fact became him, what if this could happen to anyone, even me also, an unthinkable thought, as we, my only Grandfather and I, were walking out of that futuristic new film theatre, called The Cosmonaut, in our old but still present neighbourhood in the heart of Dostoyevsky's Leningrad, as they sometimes called it on the radio (they didn't, it was my primary, *Leningrad* grandmother who did on a couple of occasions, as she liked to say odd things like that with a mysterious air, but no matter), which we, our family of four, my mother and father and me and my little brother (though not our live-in nanny Lyuba, my most favourite person in the world, to put it in a bit of a saccharine way), were about to leave forever, oh yes, forever and ever and so on, yes, in two months' time, moving out of our irregular-shaped single room in a rambling (not my word either) communal flat in the roiling heart of midtown Leningrad, Dostoyevsky was a writer apparently, here already were four Soviet cosmonauts, the only home I'd ever known in all of my almost eight years in the world, and into a three-room co-operative (whatever that, apparently very important, word meant) apartment of our own, owned by the city apparently, OK enough of that word, on Leningrad's remote southwestern edge, in the new micro-district wilderness, in *Khrushcheville*, as my parents and their friends referred to it occasionally, once or twice, chuckling, when they thought I couldn't hear them, so silly, I could hear them always, which was a cause of perennial stinging heartbreak to me, that pending self-uprooting of ours, because, well, but no, no why's, what was there even to explain, if it needed to be explained it didn't need to be explained, seeing that everything and everyone I'd ever known and loved or hated (which was one and the same thing, as my Leningrad grandmother might say with a vague smile) was in that old communal apartment, in that room, as well as at my primary school, my first grade, with my shiny red-and-gold metallic *Octoberist* star with curly-haired baby Lenin enameled in the centre of it pinned to the chest of my mousy-grey flannel uniform, in that immediate Obvodny Canal-bound neighbourhood, yes, there was no other Leningrad or any other world anywhere for me just yet, and might never be either, and Lyuba, oh Lyuba, she wasn't coming with us apparently, apparently, this was unbearable, so much so that indeed it could've been better for me never to have been born at all, OK, stop, stop, carry on carry on, although at less than eight years of age I still wasn't completely or even remotely certain about the exact, yes, to be exact, way in which I'd come to exist in the world, but OK, anyway, carry on, as the two of us, my only Grandfather, who along with my Moscow Grandmother, a school principal and teacher of Soviet human biology, had arrived earlier in Leningrad that very morning, by the posh and exclusive (many grownups called it that, and as a matter of fact, I'd already travelled by it to Moscow, twice, so there) Red Arrow overnight express train, for my mother's (their daughter's) thirty-third birthday, OK, yes, Jesus Christ never existed, which was the following day, her birthday, the last one to be celebrated in our old communal apartment, staying in a nearby-located special inn for Old Bolsheviks exclusively, of whom Grandfather most definitely was one, both old (at almost sixty, oh my) and a Bolshevik, he, seeing how distraught I was by that movie he'd taken me to see, about the contemptible traitor to the Motherland, and how outwardly scared and shaken to the metaphysical (whatever) core of my immaterial being (yes, I know, but never mind), how petrified because oh what if one's inner traitor could take seed and start growing inside anyone and everyone, everyone and their brother, although definitely of course not inside Grandfather or anyone else in our family, impossible, except maybe me, I couldn't be sure about myself, an unknown entity to myself, to put it philosophically, the regular little Hegel or Kant I was, and how big fat (OK no) tears the size of OK the size of tumour-sized poisonous mushrooms, how's that, were rolling down my something-something cheeks, put his hefty OK stop it Old-Bolshevik hand on my frail bird-like OK drop it shoulder, apparently in order to reassure me, morally to support me, to split an infinitive, telling me in a soothing soft voice that oh and I loved his raspy soft Mark Bernes-like voice, yes, but anyway, traitors to the Motherland were the worst of the worst among the scum of the Soviet earth, just the absolute worst non-people in the world, totally, hands down, bar none, none bar OK stop, and that they always but always, invariably would wind up being unmasked and brought to the ultimate measure of our swift proletarian justice in the end with a righteous Chekist bullet to the back of the traitorous head, like a dog, good riddance, inevitably and without mercy, so I didn't need to fear them, those dirty monsters, there was no reason for me to cry and tremble because of them, since they could do me no harm, silly little boy, so silly, believe you me, soothingly and softly, never oh never, cross my heart and hope, yes, my Old-Bolshevik word to you, softly and soothingly, reassuringly, reassuringly my foot, unable as he was to understand, to comprehend, OK

Grandpa I hear you, to begin to like fathom, my poor Grandfather, the true nature of my mortal despondency at that moment, for he was made of a different dough than me and there was no point trying to explain it to him, that or anything else, all the more so that I couldn't very well admit to him there might be an inner traitor growing like a deadly mushroom inside of me or he might perforce his Old-Bolshevik moral duty have to turn me in and over to the organs, out of an abundance of love for me, for my own sake and ideological and spiritual salvation, whereupon he gathered my little sweaty OK fine palm into his large and OK fine hand and led me outside, into the calm light of May noon, early afternoon it was already, the sun already was OK forget the sun, and we started walking through the valley of the OK fine the lovely it wasn't particularly beautiful but it was spacious Olympia Park first, where the aforesaid film theatre was situated, then along the apparently endless Moskovsky Prospekt, Leningrad's main transport artery, or one of the main, apparently, crowded or thronged as it was with equally and predominantly unsmiling Sunday strollers, if that's the word, the ordinary Soviet people, one or more of whom amongst that faceless multitude potentially and conceivably, inconceivably and frighteningly enough, could upon a closer look turn out to be a contemptible traitor to the Motherland or at least a carrier of that inner-traitor poisonous mushroom-ness, plodding on (the two of us) toward the imposing and so on granite structure or edifice of the venerable and whatnot Technological Institute, where my almost thirty-three year old mother incidentally had studied back in the day, as they said, before I was born, if that indeed was how I'd come about to be in the world, to become an engineer of rubber goods-making technology at the famous Red Triangle factory, right in the middle of our old and still present neighbourhood, towering over the adjective-defying Obvodny Canal's dead water the dull colour of lead, yes and of course I didn't know the word sex back at the time, nor did any of the adults in the Soviet Union either, ours was a nation of innocents, just as a tangential aside, moving on, and the entrance to the eponymous (yes, I knew many words I didn't know) metro station right there, a very important one too, a veritable transportation hub, probably not the right word apparently, as he (Grandfather) was taking me to the zoo, one of my very favourite places in the whole world OK fine, unbeknownst to me at first, as he couldn't but be sensing, likely just a projection on my part actually, that he might have gone a bit too far and had made a mistake by taking me to see that decidedly grown-up film about, well, yes, again, again, a perfectly ordinary and seemingly normal Soviet citizen suddenly and inexplicably turning out to be an unimaginable traitor to the Motherland, especially given my already vulnerable and like brittle OK no overall emotional state, of which he'd been made aware earlier in the morning by his daughter my mother, and so maybe he was trying now to make it up to me possibly, in his own grandfatherly way, additionally promising to me too, as he did on our way to the zoo down in the bottomless metro to take me afterwards to the nearest food store in that area for some, um, tomato juice, my very favourite thing to drink in the world OK fine, that fake child-speak, I swear to whatever, where in the vegetable section it was poured into thick faceted glass from an earlier era (yes, sure, I'd already heard that name, Stalin, escaping people's lips, to put it literarily, with some strange hush-hushness to their voices), from one of those giant, just very large upside-down glass cones, with coarse wet salt on the tip of that crooked aluminum teaspoon from once-white faience saucer with dark chipped edges right there, so that I could drown, so to speak, it all, drown it all, yes, my unutterable fear of possibly growing my future inner traitor inside my like being, all my inexpressible and so on sorrows in the ineffable deliciousness of our Soviet tomato juice, on the bottom of that thick-faceted Stalin-era glass, drowning and drowning and drowning, my poor Stalin-loving grandfather, futile were his naïve Old-Bolshevik efforts to cheer me up, I was utterly inconsolable, engulfed in fear and despondency, yes, one whose exact or even approximate nature was not at all clear to me OK fine, carry on, and so, after the long (for I was little and time flowed slowly through me) ride in the deservedly famed and beautiful Leningrad metro, which also was still a relatively new and therefore additionally stressful and emotionally taxing OK fine existential experience to me, there we were, there I was, yes, in my echoing inner aloneness, at the world-renowned (well, not really, but then, on the other hand, why not) Leningrad zoo, tears still welling in my OK fine, sliding down my OK fine cheeks, me doubtless looking like and indeed de facto being the most miserable child there, at the zoo, amid all the hubbub if that's the word caused by the countless (weak adjective), excitedly squealing and sleeve-tugging and so on kids of all ages, yes, including the one who was with that man we bumped into practically right upon entering, Grandfather's old friend or Party acquaintance, another Old Bolshevik, I forget the name, Grigory, yes, a tall gaunt bald man with a bony beak of a nose, a Marabou Stork, or Secretary Bird as it was known to Soviet zoo-goers (the man, not his grandson), with whom (the man, not the grandson) Grandfather immediately fell into a low-voiced yet still heated conversation about how, well, how, oh damn straight, how under Stalin there was so infinitely much more order and discipline, yes, how everything was good and radiant and idealistic and so indescribably much better than now, with all the necessary and constructive fear pervading the country's hopeful atmosphere and everywhere among the proletarian masses, when everyone's personal responsibility and accountability were literally a matter of life and death, and rightly so, in those heady no-nonsense old days of unbreakable national unity achieved through the stringent application of optimistic terror and general optimization of the warm brutality of fear, whereas now, oh now, oh what was there even to talk about, how totally depressing and altogether disgusting, all that unity was gone like apple smoke and there was no smidgen of proper respect for the Party's authority and everyone and their brother was free to snicker privately in their figurative sleeves at that foolish ass-headed traitor Nikita, don't get us started, our enemies rejoicing everywhere, as if communism-building was a laughing matter and also where pray tell was it even now, the worldwide communist revolution of their ardent youthful dreams, while in the background, issuing from an unseen megaphone behind us somewhere, the beautifully voiceless Mark Bernes, Grandfather's most beloved *estrada* performer, was singing about how, well, yes, how Russian people hated wars, couldn't abide the very idea of war, no wars ever for us, never, how could one even think otherwise, in the harrowing context of our history and but actually, come to think of it, it was the Leningrader Leonid Kostritsa singing, not Bernes, or else maybe it was Vladimir Troshin, warmly and voicelessly vocalizing the lyrics penned by the young but already internationally OK fine poet Yevgeny Evtushenko, how could anyone in the world even begin to conceive of us wanting to go to any war ever again, so totally unimaginable, and why, that Secretary-Bird man, Grigory, suddenly wanted to know, breaking away from the hushed hissing conversation about the glorious past with Grandfather and looking down at me from the stratospheric reach of his height with a benign snake-lipped smile and a touch of displeasure, why was I sniffling my nose, moping and all, wiping tears from my fearful face with the back of my hand, instead of oogling all those exotic animals and feeling happy and squealing with delight, what was wrong with me, huh, what kind of a future Young Bolshevik, haha, dedicated builder of the communism tomorrow was I going to grow up to be, haha again, just a joke, ooh such a cute little boy, be strong, little boy, don't be weak, young comrade, haha, just a joke, our enemies want you to be e=weak so you have to be strong, no joke, with Grandfather then whispering something in his ear, leaning in, all the way up there, in the rarified air of their grownup altitudes, no doubt about my being heartbroken about OK fine, and that Grigory nodded understandingly, said he understood, yes, though still looking skeptical, as we continued to move slowly from one cage with this or that animal to the next, from pen to pen, pound to pound, cesspool to cesspool, aviary to aviary, from... tiger to lion to zebra to elephant to hippo to giraffe to hyena to leopard to rhino to dik-dik to buffalo to Icelandic unicorn to full-bodied Arctic fox to the notoriously bashful Russian-taiga orangutan to the giant carnivorous frog of the Cordilleras to the winged Samoan lynx to the two-headed Tasmanian chicken and Jamaican polar bear and, well... until eventually at some point we found ourselves (or life found us) standing in front of the dark large cavernous enclo... OK, a cage is a cage is a cage, with arguably (OK who the hell talks like that) the most popular protagonist of the unfailingly and consistently cruel and gory and indeed oftentimes downright sadistic Russian folk tales, a Russian wolf in it, volk, Tambov Lupus Ordinarius, wolfie wolfie burning bright, and he was old, old, that wolf, and pitiful-looking too, raggedy, haggard, clearly deeply dispirited, broken inside, devoid of the will to live, a sad sight altogether, yes, my heart went out to him instantaneously, and indeed it was a he, volk is a male word, always a he in Russian folk tales, going ceaselessly around that terrible dark cage of his, unstoppably, unstoppably, clockwise, clockwise, ceaselessly, on and on and on and on and on, in some sort of an awful sloping limping trot, trance-like, unstoppably, round and round and round he went, not pausing even for a moment, not for a single fraction of a second, oh it was just awful, round and round and round, round and round, round and round, OK enough already probably, as if he'd gone permanently and irrevocably mad, lost his mind forever, once and for all, and mad he was of course, to be sure, although who could tell with any certainty and what was madness anyway, maybe we all were mad, our entire nation, round and round, round and round, stop stop, driven by the unendurable atavistic knowledge that he was destined to die in that cage someday too, soon too, drop dead in mid-trot, dead in the middle of one of those awful ceaseless circles around that hellacious enclosure, instant death being the only thing left for him to look forward to in life, round and round and round, and me wondering briefly about the sheer basic logistics of his very continued existence there, if and when and how he ate or slept and did he ever stop for any of that, probably not, round and round and round, feeding himself on his hopelessness, sleepless, keeping himself alive that way, despite himself, round and round, unstoppably, hypnotically, terrifyingly, heartbreakingly, OK enough already with those impotent adverbs, with the four of us standing there, in front of that cavernous cage, contemplating him in silence for what felt like a long time, me losing all track of time, for there was no time really, only timelessness, time was nothing, it was water, unable to take my eyes off him, while Grandfather and that Grigory, when at one point I did glance back up at them momentarily, regarded him with what struck me in hindsight as revulsion mixed with sadness, because probably in their eyes he represented much of everything that was wrong with the entire Soviet country, caught as it was in the deceptive mud-spattered spring of the perplexing Khrushchevian thaw, a stretch on my part perhaps, yes probably, that's the present-day me speaking, obviously, and I haven't been that boy in a lifetime, maybe never, but still, you know, maybe that's what they were thinking about just then, why not, it's all up to me to conjecture, oh the glorious ironclad monochromatic Stalinist era of their Komsomol and Party nomenklatura beginnings, those two survivors of their own youth, when many and maybe most of their comrades were being repressed arrested disappeared shot summarily with a single bullet to the back of the head for being the enemies of the people, American British Japanese spies hidden class enemies Trotskyites, you name it, ah them two poor forever deluded old Soviet Jews, long dead, long dead, what was he point of it all, as Grigory's grandson was crying disconsolately while looking and not looking at the wolf, what was that kid's name oh who cares, those two Old Bolsheviks, and of course they were younger then than I am now, who wouldn't be, but who cares, long dead, long dead, they were good people, but I was looking at the wolf, he was infinitely more important at that moment, round and round and round and round and round and round and round he went, as though trying to get rid of himself and his ravaged animal heart, round and round, what a long life it has been, as if trying to cease to exist, round and round and round, round and round, stop already, and inside me some dangerous dark ardour was growing, yes, I could tell without knowing anything about anything, the poisonous mushroom of my inner traitor, yes, and me urging and willing him to stop, stop wolf stop, if only for an instant, to have mercy on himself, telling him in a silent inner whisper that he was beautiful and I wanted to be like him, yes, I did, like him, maybe I should stop now, some things are better left unsaid, written better when not written, round and round, round and round, round and round that awful dark dank dirty cage, but then suddenly he suddenly stopped, yes, suddenly he suddenly stopped, no other way to put it, yes, he stopped suddenly and looked straight at me, well no, not true, not straight at me, not directly but obliquely, at an imperceptible angle, heavily, hopelessly, from his fierce eyes, their pupils aglow with fire and filled with fury, and no one but me seemed to have noticed... and, stunned, taken aback, feeling strangely light-headed, I asked him then, silently, in my mind, I asked him, yes, the wolf, if he could maybe let me know somehow, in some unspeakable ancient way of the wolf, if I ever, at any point in my inconceivable future, in my hopelessly heartsick life, ran the risk of becoming a traitor to the Motherland, tell me oh wolf, oh tell me, but he only smirked mirthlessly, pulling his bloodless lips away from the corners of his crimson-toothed mouth, and nodded curtly his scruffy old head with matted dark-grey fur, imperceptibly yet unmistakably, though maybe not, before resuming his ceaseless circular motion.

14

EXHALE

He told his sympathetic listener that he wasn't sure how to explain this to him, or to himself, for that matter, at this point in his life, all these decades later, but since his early twenties, he would say, and up until his permanent departure for the outer world at age thirty, he'd lived in his own country, the place of his birth, childhood and youth, the only one he'd ever known, where everyone spoke the same language as him and largely shared his so-called socio-cultural frame of reference, yes, he knew it sounded awful, but anyway, he lived there as though on an occupied territory, behind the enemy lines, in one giant area of total unpredictability, heightened risk and utter lawlessness, yes, like the Zone in the Tarkovsky film and Strugatsky Brothers' novella, and so, without quite realizing it, he'd been holding his breath continually all that time, at once loving and loathing and fearing that inescapable vast confine of his unfortunate accidental birth and subsequent childhood and youth, living with all that awful stale pent-up air in his lungs, and only letting go and exhaling finally, almost involuntarily, to the full exhaustion of his entire physical being and fairly collapsing in his seat, when the uncommonly amiable flight attendant on the plane headed for that unimaginable larger, outer world, an entire other planet unto itself, had told him, in response to his timid query, that yes, indeed, they had in fact just left the Soviet airspace, once and for all, beyond the point of no return — and the burly bartender, nodding, slid another beer to him, telling him it was on the house.

15

POSH LUST

I was sitting in an open-concept cafe of sorts (please try to be a more diligent writer, me, and have a bit more interesting openings to your stories) in a shopping mall in downtown Montreal the other day (I had a dental appointment there, then went to the pharmacy to renew a prescription, if anyone's interested), drinking my unpretentious (fake modesty detected) regular black tea, eating my delicious, refreshingly fresh (the head of the semi-underground, samizdat literary club to which I belonged back in the first half of the 1980s in Leningrad, was not far off the mark when he called me, behind my back, a literary trickster… although of course he was, too… and in any event, that's not an entirely adequate translation of the term he used then — *shtukar*, or someone who dabbles in the finery and minutiae of the craft, at the expense of overlooking the larger whole) almond croissant, scrolling through what felt like a needlessly extended and still seemingly self-perpetuating and uncontrollably burgeoning array of Russian-language Telegram channels on my phone (Trump has won, America is teetering on the brink, the world is engulfed in the most vicious Jew-hatred on my post-Soviet memory, dark days are ahead and indeed already upon us, and I felt at the moment I needed a break from any and all anglophone political content), that bottomless mixed bag of real horror and pure silliness, sadness and cringeworthy pretentiousness, raw heartbreak, cruelty and disbelief, cautious mindfulness and outright denial, relentless virtue-signaling and rare searing honesty, breathtaking stupidity and reluctant objectivity, self-righteousness, brutal honesty and triumphant *poshlost* (that gross spiritual tackiness whose incomprehensibly elusive nature of a randomly semi-invisible and unpredictably shape-shifting Russian butterfly from hell that matchless classifier of the ineffable, Vladimir Nabokov, who, apropos of nothing, shared, with a future-bound interval of twenty-nine years, a birthday with his polar antipode and overall a fairly uniquely evil man, Vladimir Lenin, had attempted repeatedly and largely unsuccessfully to pin down, referring to it by turns as "corny trash, vulgar clichés, Philistinism in all its phases, imitations of imitations, bogus profundities," and, of course, famously, "posh-lust" — indeed, that overpowering sublimated noxious, sickeningly narcissistic and self-destructive, ugly insatiable lust for the vapid poshness of constant mass attention and either adoration or hatred, it doesn't matter which, so long as one remains firmly lodged in the dead centre of popular attention and keeps being mentioned, talked about, talked about, no matter the cost, no matter what it takes, no matter how many people may get hurt in the process of one's trying to fill that bottomless vortex of inner need… what an unimaginable price America and the world have already paid and still are going to pay for Trump's posh lust for life, but…) — in other words, I was minding my own little solitary business of biding my time, doing nothing, idling away, being inconspicuous, while waiting for my prescription to be filled at the pharmacy to the right and a bit down the way at the mall (nothing serious, if anyone's interested, although in truth, I'm not sure I know what the purpose of my still living may be, yes, to be frank with you, I'm not being coy, maybe just a little, it's like a patient asking a doctor whether he is going to live and the doctor replies by saying, well, perhaps, but what would be the point), yes, mulling over on the periphery of my mind the dreadful posh lust of Trump's life, while perusing those Russian Telegram channels (so much angst, so much silliness, so much… and oh, a message from someone I didn't even know popping up on the screen, warning me that he, the correspondent, had read my Facebook posts and if I thought Trump was not going to get me in Canada, well, I had another think coming… how do you like them apples, the world is awash in vileness and stupidity… posh lust, posh lust) and kind of musing also abstractly about all the stories I'd promised myself (well, not *promised* promised, but… let me just say that those might be the reason, to my own silly mind, of my continued existence) I would and should and ought to have written by now if not for the posh lust of existential entropy (aka laziness and paralyzing indecisiveness… having been frozen into non-writing by having too many stories to write) intervening (I'll try to be brief here, in this next passage, because there can hardly be anything less interesting and more annoying to the hypothetical reader to deal with in a literary text than writers' smug commiserations about the posh lust of their writerly despondencies), such as one about Richard Nixon unwittingly (well, duh) intervening with my prospective and theretofore nonexistent love life of an almost-seventeen year-old back in Leningrad, or one about how at one feverish point on one keenly memorable night in early September of the year 1972 in a tiny dirt-spattered log cabin with sloping earthen floor in a remote (some two hundred-plus kilometres due north-east from Leningrad) village, much to my instant piercing horror the seventeen-year-old me, a naïve Jewish kid from an upper-middle-class Soviet family, suddenly discovered my deep-seated anti-Soviet essence, or one about my cousin from Moscow (the greatest and most beloved friend of my childhood and adolescence) and me going crawfish-hunting in the shallow water of the beautiful Karelian lake at my family's dacha, some one hundred-plus kilometres from the city, on the late-June white night of the Soyuz-11 spaceship tragedy (Dobrovolsky-Volkov-Patsaev… we brought two full aluminum buckets full of crawfish back to the cabin and boiled and ate those critters with two bottles of beer, to my grandmother's feigned displeasure, and talked about the clearly and suddenly irrevocably divergent paths of our future), or one about… but oh, so many, so infinitely and impossibly many of them, a veritable Karelian lake's worth of stories waiting helplessly to be written, probably in vain, too, so damn many, oh so… oh stop whining and moaning, me, and now I'm in the twilight of my life, oh, so sad, shut up already, *poshlyak* (someone mired and marinated in poshlost), and at this point I may not even feel any more like reminiscing about my Russian childhood and youth, now that Russia is probably the main link in the world's axis of evil, a full-fledged fascist state, but what can I do, I can't stop the war in Ukraine, I can't depose Putin, I can't do this or that and the other, I'm a nobody (oh, look who thinks he's no one), I'm just an old former Soviet Jew, I'm not a revolutionary, much less a great hero like Navalny, I'm just a writer of unwritten stories, and sometimes late at night I sit up in bed, panting, stop it, knowing I'll never again see St. Petersburg, the city of my life, OK, this is posh lust, don't be a poshlyak, posh lyak, what in hell is a lyak, am I a lyak or just an idiot (incidentally, as one of the five or six first-place co-winners in all-Leningrad inter-high school literary contest administered by the venerable, Palace of Pioneers-affiliated literary club *Derzanie* (Dare) — my final essay in that three-stage affair, penned on the spot, in one six-hours sitting, in a large, quietly sun-dappled auditorium at the august Herzen Pedagogical University, under the personal auspices of the late great Savely Izraelevich Fridman, in another lifetime, in the lovely, promise-laden spring of the fifty-fifth anniversary of the Great October Socialist Revolution of 1917, yes, the same year again, 1972, was a twenty-page comparative essay on the Russian translation of Robert Penn Warren's novel *All the King's Men* and the eponymous Soviet TV-serial based on it, and that specific topic was of my own impromptu choosing — I received a memorable honorary prize in the form of an elegant, deluxe new academic edition of Fyodor Mikhailovich Dostoyevsky's novel *The Idiot*), and now I've also remembered something else, on a similar subject of my identity, yes, how, some time ago, on a plane from somewhere to someplace else, I was jotting down something doubtless transcendentally existential and altogether eternal (we had just experienced some unsettling and fleetingly terrifying turbulence) in my pocket notebook, when the somewhat nondescript man sitting next to me, either bored or, well, bored, leaned in my way and asked, rather out of nowhere, if I was some kind of writer maybe, and I told him politely that one probably could say that, in a manner of speaking, or maybe one could not, and so, not quite unexpectedly, the next thing he wanted to know was whether I'd written something he might have read, and then, in response, I turned the notebook page and wrote, in VERY large letters, N O, and showed the page to him, adding that yes he sure had, now he had, and we both kind of laughed, although he seemed nonplussed, and… but back to that caffe at the mall where, instantly pulling me out of the doldrums of my dolorous musings, a possibly inebriated or else harmlessly mad but generally decent-looking man, probably in his fifties or early sixties, strikingly well-dressed, wearing a double-breasted camel wool coat and sporting a red cashmere scarf and, imagine, a Borsalino fedora hat, straight out of the eponymous old Alain Delon movie, lowered himself down on a chair directly across from me at the empty and pretty darn long table (I gave him a coldly puzzled look, with a shoulder-shrug of a question in my eyes), smiled at me beatifically, and uttered, in a pleasantly melodious, sweetly warbling voice, something entirely nonsensical that, to my auditory perception at least, sounded like "Ich habe nicht ein doodley doodley dan" — to which, upon an understandable split-second pause (somewhere in back of me, a phone rang, crooning out in a soulful falsetto, "Ooh baby baby, ooh baby baby"), I reciprocated accordingly, by proceeding to relate to him, over the following five minutes or so and in the warm glow of his unflagging attention, the full and unabridged story of my ill-starred life.

16

RAIN

Sometimes just listening to the rain all night is enough.

17

NAIROBI RAIN

Rain, rain outside, in pre-dawn Nairobi, stubbornly unstoppable, monotonous, relentless, like the unending yet somehow comforting and reassuring autumn rains of my Leningrad childhood and youth.

18

BIRDS

Birds are chirping like crazy, like a legion of lovelorn crickets just outside my window, in the dead of winter, amid all that snow, what do they know?

19

I AM

I am, I exist, I am not a figment of my own or anyone else's imagination, no way, I am standing there, under the blue sky of my eight-year-old world, this is a bit too cutely put maybe, feeling the soft hesitant wind on my there needs to be an adjective here skin, seeing shadows of shadows, sharp-edged sunny spaces, on a benign mid-September Leningrad afternoon, *Lemmingrad* I just typed out blindly, the city of lemmings, moving on, I am not a blind typist but I am a near-sighted one, this is a bit too cutely put also, don't get carried away, womenfolk's summer this lovely stretch of early fall is called in Russia, *bab'ye leto*, which is like a watercolour of itself, the afternoon is, not sure about that image, a bit too cute by half perhaps, let's start again, no, let's not, I am eight years and two months old, I was born and live in Leningrad, my parents recently told me that I'm a Jew, all of us are, a heartbreaking life-altering bit of information, yes, I'm so ashamed of myself, that's not who or what I want to be, if I could just cease to exist I would, not entirely true, yes it is, but that would be the optics I hate that word of an adult an old man looking back, moving on, standing aimlessly, lost momentarily in the fearsome, not the right adjective, sheer strangeness of my utterly insignificant moving on minuscule existence in this vast and raw new world of my unhappy being, this is too cute by half, at the outbound end of the poorly asphalted, dirt-spattered narrow passageway separating our nondescript and of course that wouldn't be a word from my vocabulary as an eight year-old, moving on, apartment building from its exact five-story concrete-box replica, lookalike squarely across the way somewhere in the spatially undefinable whatever middle of a fast-growing, or so they say, but I can see it with my own eyes too, micro-district, yes, *Khrushcheville* as my parents and their friends occasionally refer to it with a bemused chuckle when assuming or presuming themselves to be outside of my earshot, this is too cute by half, on Leningrad's remote southwestern edge, where our family of four was finally and much to my heartbreak and lingering sadness, it's not an either or situation, granted by the competent municipal authorities' permission, I already know a little English, to relocate earlier in the year and indeed has moved to two weeks ago, yes, unbelievably, oh believe it, exchanging the cozily cramped this is too cute by half moving on confines of our single room in the rambling communal apartment in the roiling Dostoyevskean drop that don't use that word ever again core of the great entirely unrepeatable city for the unimaginable hateful luxury too many loud adjectives of the thirty-four square metres' worth of a three-room space of our own, although strictly speaking it is not ours, it's the city's, the municipality's, our entire nation's, oh I miss our room in that old communal apartment, I miss my life as it used to be, before everything, before I became so ashamed of myself, I miss living there in that room with my parents and my little brother and our live-in nanny Lyuba, the eternal love of my early childhood, this may be too cutely put, yes, she has not moved into our new place with us, exiting my life forever, too cute by half, too soap-operatic, where is she now and will I ever see her again, almost certainly not, such losses, moving on, life is all about one loss after another, *Lossel* is how they often spell my last name as a grownup an old man a middle-aged man an old man, especially in Kenya, too long to explain, Kenya, some other time, life happened, a man of losses, as if they didn't know last names normally start with a capital letter, oh well, it's my own fault, admittedly, for I should've spelled my name with a Y not I when applying for a green card upon arrival in America, all these decades ago, but, but what, but nothing, I just didn't want to be at the very end of every alphabetical list I would ever end up being on in America, I suppose, so there, such shallow reasoning, so ashamed of myself, stop saying that, I miss everyone in that old communal apartment in our old midtown neighbourhood, in the roiling Dostoyevskean oh drop it, even the ever-angry, furious even, yes, firaly and inexplicably seething with anger at all times, vicious and vile yet probably and possibly kind-hearted too, deep down inside, very deep, extremely, Old Faina, her in her old Army boots who moving on, I don't want to think of her now, don't miss her enough, don't miss her at all, and now that I know that I am a Jew and am supposed to want nothing more in the world than to harm the good kind eternally trustful Russian people and all other people too for good measure and that I was the one who crucified Jesus Christ, who doesn't exist, now that I know that everyone in the world knows, then what, then nothing, shame shame shame,

OK, moving on, I miss other children my age in that apartment, also my fellow first-graders, this is too cute by half, they are all in the second grade now obviously, from my old school on Fifth Red Cavalry street, five-minute walk from our old Dostoyevskean stop it apartment building, built in another century, under the tsarist regime, moving on, before the Great October Socialist Revolution, this is too cute by half, my grandfather is an old Bolshevik, he used to deify and idolize Stalin or so I've heard being said, whispered, Stalin was a man of steel, I miss everything and everyone, knowing it will be forever, an impossible concept for an eight year-old to grasp, especially that girl from my first-grade class, now in the second grade there, Larissa, yes, I walked her home once after school, with her, once, after school, shadows and sunshine, trembling sun-filled spiderweb silences of midtown streets, she invited me to her apartment, the one on Fourth Red Cavalry Street, a single-family apartment, not a communal one, imagine, man of losses, man of losses, until then I hadn't known anyone living in a single apartment, except my grandmother's older brother and his wife and their three children, all older than me, and their nanny, Gasha, Lyuba's aunt, also from Cheboksary, capital of the Volga-bound Chuvash Autonomous Soviet Socialist Republic, along with my grandmother and great-grandmother, all of them in that very large old flat on Sixth Red Cavalry Street, with a whole room specifically designated as Library there, with lots of books in it, such as the fifty-two dark-blue volumes of the Great Soviet Encyclopedia, what wouldn't I give to be back there now, as a child, and even some books in English, some of them, moving on, but also of course, my Moscow grandparents, I only have one grandfather, an old Bolshevik, living in a spacious or airy or some such word single-family apartment in the suburbs of Moscow, Moose Island it's called, yes, moving on, I also lived there for a year, with them, my Moscow grandparents, between the ages of six and seven, this is too formally put, too starchily, so very recently and a lifetime away, moving on, I'm just standing there, so ashamed of myself, man of losses, man of steel, yes, and I don't know, I have no idea, as I'm standing there, at the end of that I don't know how to put it passageway, OK, where the latter moving on intersects with the nominally very superficially practically not paved at all road leading from Cosmonauts Avenue, where we live, that's our new address, oh how I don't want to be there, cut the soap opera, what a desolate place, dolorous, to Yuri Gagarin Avenue, where my new grade-to-high school is situated, not sure that's the right word, where I've only been going for one week so far, moving on, and where I am the forty-third pupil in the Second-D class, yes I am, in a room that can hardly fit in more than twenty kids, little Soviet Leningrad children in mousy-grey uniforms and nondescript brown dresses or whatever, so we're all sitting three or four to a desk there, in that classroom, which is ridiculous, but then no one there knows yet that I'm a Jew, oh you really think so, haha, don't be ridiculous, the teachers know, all of them, others also, and how about looking at yourself in the mirror, any mirror of your choice anyplace, at the size and shape of your nose, say, and didn't someone already sneer at you on the street in the old neighbourhood just before the move and called you by the name your parents had warned you you would from time to time well regularly be called for the rest of your life, now that I know who I am, I don't know who I am, moving on, so ashamed, moving on, man of losses, just standing there, where from the window of your and your little brother's room you can see nothing but an endless expanse of industrial wasteland, as far as the eye can see, nothing but liquid not sure that's the right word mud cratered and dotted with tectonic lakes, the sovereign habitat cut it out of water rats that I've seen local boys older than me hunt from their makeshift rafts with their long sticks with long rusted forks attached to them, gigs those were called, moving on, I don't know in that moment if I'll ever see Larissa again, although we'll still be living in the same city, technically speaking, technically, yet she could just as well be on another planet, get used to it, man of losses, so I'm standing there, aimlessly, on a typically benign womenfolk's-summer afternoon, feeling heartbroken OK don't be overdoing it and looking at this enormous expanse of nothingness in front of me, surrounding me on all sides, from every direction, liquid mud, liquid mud, and believe it or not, for a briefest of instants a joyful feeling enters my insignificant little being or whatever, because the sun, because I'm alive, simple as that, trite as it may sound, who cares, and all this fierce ferocious raw strangeness, this terrible and beautiful world, because life is endless, this unending open space of life, this is too cute by half, moving on, constantly shifting perspectives, then just as quickly it is gone, as I'm still thinking of Larissa, of how she told me, when we were drinking tea from the faience cups of imperial make, her benighted what does that word mean grandmother told us proudly, imperial, yes, what the hell, my Old Bolshevik grandfather wouldn't like her or anyone using that word, that she had a boyfriend, Larissa did, man of losses, in the parallel first grade at that old school, named Dima, oh eff me, eff my life, whose father was a damn lawyer, what was that, or at the very least she liked him, why are you telling me this, Larissa, Larissa, which is why she was calling him her boyfriend, which is one and the same thing and I feel like dying, get over yourself, moving on, and I am moving on, even as I'm standing there, aimlessly, feeling I've already lived a life that's been too damn long, endless, it's interminable, really, eight years, my god, I didn't say that word even in my mind, what would be the point of extending or prolonging this sadness any further, farther, further, father, father, this meaninglessness and stuff, this is too cue by half, man of losses, man of steel, and I'm imagining myself with pleasure being dead, laying sad and stern and with my hollow eyes closed this is awkwardly put moving on and oh so impossibly stop it handsome, whatever, in a coffin made of old oak or some other noble kind of wood, red or black, red and black, like Lenin's tomb in Red Square, his mausoleum, been there, with everyone standing around the be-coffined me being totally heartbroken, utterly, filled with unbearable remorse, Larissa in particular with her nominal boyfriend lawyer's son named Dima and everyone saying through tears sobbing out how we so underappreciated him me he was too good for us and for this ugly cruel world oh he was a real genius of a child and potentially the greatest human being ever to walk the earth but we but we oh but us but we were so blind shame on us but he was a Jew but that's OK still OK moving on and everyone feeling crushed, totally and completely, standing around my coffin, moving on, and I feel sorry for them, but what can I do, I'm dead, and my parents saying to each other, through veritable torrents of tears, we shouldn't have moved him from that old communal apartment to this you know wild wilderness, it was a tragic blunder of cosmic proportions on our part, how could we have been so unforgivably insensitive to his feelings, his emotional needs, and now it's too late too late, too late, I run those two words, too late, in my mind, over and over again, as I'm lying there, laying, in that beautiful coffin, too late too late too late *slishkom pozdno slishkom pozdnoslish kompozdnnoslish*, with steadily increasing acceleration because how else would I occupy myself there, in that stupid coffin, this whole being dead thing is getting old on me, until they start blurring into and unto each other, those two words, too late, resembling some ominous sinister incantation echoing inside my head, words blurring together, *slishkom pozdnoslish kompozdnoslishkompozdno kompozdno dno dno dnodnodno*, OK, moving on, but where is everyone, why am I the only one there, how odd, why can't I see anyone, a solitary man of losses in this wasteland surrounding me, have Americans dropped an atomic bomb on us or something, considering that typically it is relatively quick with people, if that's the word, with all the new micro-district dwellers, newcomers, re-settlers like us here, OK, maybe it's Sunday and so that's why, but I don't think so, but then, if it's not Sunday and it is afternoon, which it is, then why am I not at school, huh, that's a good question, no idea, moving on, it doesn't matter,

I'm still alive, all these lifetimes later, and I have a feeling I've existed forever, although of course I'm not him, that sad and confused little Leningrad boy, while from an open window somewhere nearby, one of the exact same five-story concrete-block boxes of apartment buildings that comprise the entirety of our new neighbourhood, our *Khrushcheville* micro-district, I can hear the soft, ruminative, sad, beautiful cut it out "voiceless," as my Moscow grandmother calls it, voice of Mark Bernes, my grandfather's voiceless singing idol singing about how Russian people don't want war, totally not, never, are you kidding, and we don't, we don't want war, although I'm a Jew, strictly speaking, at least nominally so, and so is my grandfather and so is Mark Bernes, but not Evgeny Evtushenko, the poet the author of the lyrics, no, not him, of course I know who he is, we the Soviet people we the Soviet people we the Soviet people, we are good we are good oh so very good, hush-hush baby, we are the light of the world and America its ugly darkness, historically doomed, the world of imperialism is, even if it decides to drop its atomic bomb on us, in which case it's not really terrible to die along with everyone else, yes, our entire nation, it would be like living along with everyone else, no difference, although I'll admit I'm a little scared, yes, because me being dead is still a new idea to me and, well, as though in order to assuage my fears, this is too cute by half, to be rephrased later, if there is one, that later, to calm me down and soothe my nerves and my immortal soul and comfort me and whatnot, from another direction, but also somewhere very close by, from some other window in our new apartment building, comes the heavenly and a bit nauseatingly even lovely saccharine lyrical tenor of the greatest opera singer alive and, well, OK, my Leningrad grandmother, my father's mother, who lives now in the same apartment building with us, only we're on the third floor and she and great-grandmother on the first with their fat colicky old black cat Kuzya and, in short, she always says Ivan Kozlovsky's voice is just heavenly, although that does not imply that heaven exists, or hell either, everyone knows there is no god, everyone that is except Lyuba, my forever love, whom I may never see again, along with Larissa, but Lyuba more so, she doesn't have a boyfriend, moving on, Lyuba believed in god, still does no doubt, wherever she is now, it was our secret, she knew I could tell on her at any moment, betray her in effect, if I were a stranger to myself, someone I didn't know I was, but then I am a Jew, it turns out, so who knows, a snake doesn't know it's a snake, and I am supposed to wish nothing but evil on the good and gullible Russian people, but I don't, I don't think I do, I love Lyuba, and then she would've been be in a world of trouble, had I old on her, that she had an image of an icon or whatever looked like my mother that woman under her bed no in her old suitcase among her clothes, and so now Kozlovsky, moving on, is singing what I know to be Lensky's aria from the opera *Evgeny Onegin*, and who pray tell are those two, Onegin-Lensky, and the latter is wondering, via Kozlovsky, as to where they have gone, the golden days of his spring, this is too cute by half, and for an instant I have a feeling he's singing about me, Kozlovsky is, because even at my eight years of age, I know I've already lived an impossibly don't overdo it long life and the golden days of my spring are already behind me possibly and now I'm in the this is too cute by half September of my life, with Kozlovsky now channeling Lensky's anguished musings with regard to what the coming day would have in store for the him, a good question, Lensky, and the answer to it unfortunately is nothing good, yes, unfortunately or fortunately, and whether he would be killed dead by the deadly arrow, what arrow who uses arrows anymore, while out of nowhere, it seems, two big boys, probably middle-schoolers already, at least twelve or fourteen or maybe even forty years old each, this is too cute by half, materialize practically right in front of me, in the distance, mirage-like, walking briskly in the direction of Cosmonauts Avenue, which is right behind me, from the Yuri Gagarin Avenue's emptiness five minutes' worth of OK, moving on, and they are talking animatedly, discussing probably the upcoming football match between us, our Soviet team and Hungary, Hungary is strong, I know, I love football, football, not soccer, man of losses, man of losses, man of steel, moving on, I can name almost all the players in the major league, despite the general pointlessness of my existence, moving on, and then one of the boys, for no reason at all, asks the other in English, in English for no reason, once they're within my earshot, what his name is, in English, and the other boy responds by saying his name is John, the two burst out laughing, and the first boy says his name is Jack, still laughing, now the two are practically doubling over with laughter, slapping each other's backs and all that sort of tomfoolery and horsing around, moving on, yes I already know English a little, grandmother's older brother's aforementioned apartment on Sixth Red Cavalry Street has all those books in English there in its mind-boggling Library room, as his wife is a college teacher of English, and those books in English they have there are a lot of fun to look at, to put it mildly, like the one that is a book of American cartoons published in nineteen-thirties, with Mickey Mouse and Donald Duck, and also one from around the beginning of the century, published in England, so very strange, and it's about England, too, titled *This is England*, and when I'm in that room I have to keep reminding myself that imperialism is historically doomed, there're many old poems I cannot read and other such texts in that book, I can read none o them, to be honest, but also lots of old photographs and drawings of London, so I already know a little English, maybe more than a little, I just don't know how well or poorly I know it, I only know a few words, realistically speaking, and these boys, they clearly are on their way home, maybe they're brothers, who cares, from an English lesson at school, which means they must already be like in eighth grade or so, man alive, or maybe they're studying English at the Young Pioneers Palace over on the Nevsky, which I have never seen actually, the palace, not the Nevsky, although the Nevsky either, if truth be told, in all of my eight years in this world, maybe just a couple of times with my parents, probably, although I've heard a lot about it, the palace, not the Nevsky, but the Nevsky also, it's my whole life, my Leningrad, it's everyone's main street, it's the main symbol of our belonging, our very existence, there is no Leningrad without the Nevsky, moving on, they probably and undoubtedly well sure also have just moved to this new micro-district of ours from somewhere else in Leningrad, no kidding, good thinking, and finally they notice me and stop momentarily, as if I were such a very startling spectacle, a mirage unto myself, with one of them then saying loudly that he sees a boy, in English, and the other responding to the effect that he is seeing not just any boy but a little boy, a little boy with a big nose, and they both starting to laugh again, like two damn Neanderthals or something, then one of them addresses me directly, saying A little boy, do you speak English, yes, all of a sudden, *doo eweyooo spik Inglizh*, in this aggressive tone, startling me quite a bit, my heart starting to beat very rapidly in my chest, to hammer away in my ears, deafening me momentarily, so that I almost cannot breathe, moving on, and so I say to him, also loudly, but no, tremulously, in a pathetic broken weak high-pitched voice full of impotent defiance, Yes I am, yes, that's what I say in response to that question, *YES I AM*, already knowing even before closing my mouth that I've screwed it up in some fundamental way and will never be forgiven, never will be able to live it down, as the two big boys fairly holler with delight upon hearing that, almost literally falling down all over themselves in an overload of cruel merriment, jumping up and down and splashing around that disgusting liquid mud beneath our feet, just roaring with laughter, come on it's too much it's not that big a deal apparently it is, repeating to each other Yes I am, Yes I am, but then stopping abruptly and looking at me with cold derision and pure contempt, and saying to me, one or both of them at once, A little boy, you speak English not, yes, and already losing interest in me, my tiny persona altogether, starting to move away, walking ever faster, resuming their progress towards Cosmonauts

Avenue, leaving me behind in the mud, standing there, as shame unfurls in my chest like a searingly hot bright red flower, burning me to death from within, this shame, this fire inside me, killing me softly on the spot, forever and without any hope of redemption, oh the things we remember, man of losses, fool fool fool fool fool fool fool fool fool.

20

SPRINGS ETERNAL

Everything that can go wrong will go wrong, you'll make yourself look and sound like a fool, you'll be a wild-eyed mess, you'll fail the ultimate test of your professional career, you'll have your phone stolen or it'll slip from your hand and fall in the azure ocean below a beautiful tall bridge, oh well, insert your own private nightmare here, none of won't scar you, you'll lose the person you thought was the love of your life, you'll feel hopeless and disoriented, you'll become convinced you've wasted your life, you'll get depressed as hell, you'll question the very purpose of and rationale for your continued existence, you'll drink too much maybe, you'll spend a lot of time laying on your bed facing the wall with your eyes open, you'll... oh, what else can I tell you, you'll get sick of yourself eventually, but you'll snap out of it, finish this sorrowful passage as you see fit, of course it will be all right in the end, how can it not, it's just life and death will just be death, noting to fear or think about too hard, and it's not all about you, and even on the very bottom of despondency you'll know there are people who still love you and... and that is true actually, and you'll realize that hopelessness or whatever you call it is but the ground zero of hope, which springs eternal, springs eternal, springs eternal...

21

KINDERGARTEN

I am four and tiny of size, and I don't know why I don't want to go to kindergarten, for the first time ever, ruining my parents' vital plans, I just don't, and to say that I don't want to go would really be saying nothing, for I am absolutely terrified, petrified, beyond myself with mortal despondency, undone, crushed to death by boundless panic, big fat tears streaming down my face with a distorted gaping mouth, a gaping mouth of a face, which must be very red, crimson and shining, as my mother is trying in vain, in a pleading and threatening and cajoling voice, to convince and persuade me and reason with me and mollify me, all the while attempting with steadily decreasing gentleness to pull me out onto the stairwell landing, into the ominous outside world, through the front door of our rambling communal apartment, the poor frantic discombobulated confused exasperated frightened Soviet Jewish woman, not yet thirty years of age, an engineer-technologist at the world-famous rubber-goods factory called Red Triangle, on the other side of the ghastly Obvodny Canal from us, Leningrad's main open-air sewage artery, but to no avail, no avail, nothing doing, sorry mom, no way, not going to happen, not going to kindergarten, I'd rather be dead, literally so, yes, although of course no, so what can she do short of hurting me physically, which she's not about to do, she's not succeeding, my poor mother, just a girl really, I won't be going to no damn kindergarten, I mean it, I don't know why but I won't, I'd sooner throw myself into the vertiginous abyss of the stairwell shaft, we live on the sixth floor, it's a massive pre-revolutionary, tsarist-era Dostoyevsky's-Petersburg apartment building, very tall echoing flights of stairs, and I am screaming and wailing like fire-engine siren from Samuil Marshak's book-length children's poem called *The Fire*, oh I love the painted pictures in it, all those cozy old tall granite apartment buildings lapped greedily at by tongues of fire, causing my poor mother to become totally desperate, she'll be late for work, because if I don't go to kindergarten, then our live-in Nanny Lyuba, my favourite, yes, that's the world, person in the world, who is living in Leningrad illegally, plus she believes in god secretly (but I'm not going to rat her out, I love her), yes, if I don't go to kindergarten, then she'll have to take care of the two of us, my little brother and me, which she may not be able to handle, simply in terms of her normal physical workload, since I just had a baby brother less than one year ago, nobody asked me if I wanted one but that's fine, I like him, and there is no room in our single room in our communal apartment for all the five of us, me and my baby brother and my parents and Lyuba, yes, my very favourite person in the world, an illiterate or maybe not very literate sixteen year-old girl from the Volga-bound Chuvash Autonomous Soviet Socialist Republic and its capital Cheboksary, so maybe I don't want to see Lyuba taking care of my baby brother, instead of me or along with me, I want her undivided love and attention, maybe I simply am jealous, is that what it's all about, sure, probably, but that's a conjecture on my part, although likely a correct one, so yes, my mother is in a real bind, both my parents are, for there is no room for all of us in our single irregularly shaped room in our rambling and messy communal apartment, don't even get me started on the subject, although I've been started already, kind of, but I don't want to comprehend the situation we're in, Lyuba-wise, space-wise, don't want to listen to my mother's pleadings and threats, her pitiful small voice of reason, no, I'm wailing like a fire engine, feeling as if my life were ending, as though my very life force were seeping out of me, like sands through the hourglass, yes, so I keep screaming and howling at the top of my lungs, blabbering and blubbering, speaking in tongues, so to speak, or maybe I'm screaming and shouting because I'm trying to communicate to her and the entire musty and angry world of our communal apartment and the stairwell landing outside that I don't want to live in the Soviet Union, that's right, oh that's a good one, that I'm deeply unhappy to have been born in a totalitarian state, with my quick inquisitive mind and my presumable talent for whatever, that communism is historically doomed, yes, doomed, at four years of age I have already been able to come to that extremely risky philosophical conclusion, OK, cut it out, and maybe, and most likely, I'm so beyond myself and my very existence just now, in these interminable moments, because I'm feeling that if she and the world do succeed in overpowering me, if I do let my mother and the world drag me out onto that cold-stoned stairwell landing (and some of the people living in our communal apartment at this point are standing behind her in the tenebrous, if that's the right adjective, perspective of the endless dark communal corridor, their faces gloomy and indistinct, while at the same time starkly disapproving, a somber forest of grown-ups), well, so, yes, if she does manage to pull or push or drag me out onto the landing and then down all those flights of stairs and out into the cavernous inner courtyard and out into the street, through that dank lightless archway there, and finally to the kindergarten gates, about two- or five- or ten-minute walk away, then my life would effectively be over, rendered completely void of meaning, my life as I got to know it so far, in the sense that it will begin in earnest then, will stir into irrevocable motion, irreversible things will start happening in and to it, it will be like stepping into a deceptively placid river with a powerfully strong undercurrent, and people that I love will start moving rapidly and unstoppably toward old age and dying, yes, if only I let her, let them, permit myself to be taken to those massive cast-iron kindergarten gates, but that too is a conjecture, a supposition, just a fancy literary whatever on my part, hypothesis maybe, my mind is like a restless and harrowed and haunted and gaunt caged animal (yes, too many adjectives, obviously), a wolf in the Leningrad Zoo or some such animal, restless and extremely tired, just so damn tired, man, already, even at my age, before my life has even begun properly, so no, no, I won't go, no, forgive me mother, please, and now I'm just wheezing and croaking and rasping, coughing, as if there was a hairball of horror stuck in my Adam's apple-less throat, which scares my mother, I can tell, or I would imagine so, so now she in turn is tiring and weakening and despairing, seeing as she must be that this is something quite serious happening with or to her son, not just your garden-variety temper tantrum but something that cannot be reasoned with in any ordinary way or along any recognizable behavioural patterns, that there clearly can be no pacifying me for as long as she and all of them are persisting in her determination to… and so on, never, never, this is bigger than me, bigger than her, bigger than all of us, a fateful moment (I wouldn't be able to express this in words, which means it's a true feeling), and so, yes... with a sobbing sigh she gives up and leads me back into our infinitely familiar irregularly shaped single room, where besides the five of us there is also father's massive desk, because he is a promising and already almost prominent young scientist in the strictly-classified field of submarine electromagnetism, plus the old Red October piano, discordant but no matter, a piano is a piano, and then also my parents' bed and my little brother's, what's the word I'm looking for here, manger, yes, and my small well-worn fold-out couch and Lyuba's roll-out mattress on the floor (she believes in god, in secret, it is our secret, I'm not ratting her out), and what do you know, all of a sudden there is peace again in my tormented four-year-old soul, unless I existed before I came into the world in some mysterious way, everything is right with the world (nothing is, but no matter), yes, and then, shortly thereafter, a few weeks later, instead of the kindergarten, my parents send me off to live with my grandparents in Moscow, for a year, in the quiet remote suburb called Moose Island, where I somehow promptly get a potentially fatal infection in my lower jaw and nearly die in the local Moose Island hospital, while feeling completely unafraid and upbeat about the whole situation, and even unnaturally joyous, but that already is a whole other story.

22

NO KEKULE

Sometimes — infrequently but not never — in your dream you suddenly are presented, right in front of the inner side of your eyelids, with a brightly lit, wavering slightly in place, as if teasing you, page of something you supposedly have just written, unbeknownst to yourself; and the writing there, on that page is so perfect, so incomparably better that anything you've ever been able to compose in your non-dream life, that, both elated and pre-emptively heartbroken at once (because not even too deep down, below the uneasy surface of your dream-mind, you know that whoever may have put those words together, it wasn't you, it was your subconscious, yes, of course, which is infinitely wiser than you and knows you a million times better than you ever would begin to know yourself, and it is trying right now to help you, out of the goodness of its nonexistent heart and in its own inimitable way), and you start frantically trying in your sleep to commit it, that page, to the elusive parallel memory of your dream-life, in the illusory hope that it might be kind enough to deposit it somehow by morning into the prefrontal cortex or amygdala of your non-dormant self, while also hoping against hope to wake up that very moment, so that you could, still half-asleep, shuffle over to your desk in the dark and find a pen and a piece of paper there, to jot down that dream-text, like some kind of Kekule of writing — but alas, neither of those two desperate dream-wishes ever come true, for you are no damn Kekule…

23

GOOGLE GULAG

When Professor N (or just Professor, like the luckless protagonist of that famous Paul Bowles story he's never read whose title escaped him momentarily) first noticed, stoically unalarmed (life takes its toll, you know, time catches up with you, it's useless to rebel against time, so it goes), that his mind — theretofore, objectively speaking, the most reliable or whatever asset of his rather depressingly long and, if truth to be told, only moderately distinguished academic career — had started slipping, faltering, stumbling upon nothing but the empty space of… no, he couldn't recall, betraying him at random moments unignorably, in short beginning to have increasingly frequent difficulty recollecting this or that iconic name or literary title in his field and or and refusing to come up with seemingly the least forgettable of the only and naturally and organically right words during a lecture (seminar, rather, always a seminar), he had in response no other recourse but to start implementing some ("A Remote Incident" maybe… no) necessarily uncomplicated and indeed touchingly naive (not from his perspective, of course) strategies for like working his light-footed and yada-yada way around those, always unforeseeable just a split second in advance, potholes, or apnea, say what, of meaning, of all those suddenly missing words and

("A Faraway Occurrence" perhaps… no) essential names and salient titles and quotes, as nimbly and *unhiccupingly* inconspicuously as possible, replacing all the aforesaid on the spot with their reasonably close paraphrastic periphrastic allusive parabolic approximations and synonyms plucked out of the rarified air of his vestigial lingual memory of... uh… an immigrant to English (yeah, OK, that's right, that's the ticket, let's posit and stipulate, for greater narrative serendipity's sake, that he came to the US from the former Soviet Union about forty years ago, good God, and that he is a college professor of — what else — the currently severely unfashionable and generally and deservedly oh give me a break frowned upon Russian literature in the department of Slavic-slash-Eastern-European Studies at an upscale and selective private liberal arts college in an economically woebegone (you ain't no Garrison Keillor… Senator) mid-size city in upstate New York, and that his specific area of research — research-shmersearch, my butt — is the literary samizdat scene in 1970–'80s Leningrad, sure, of course, what else, but obviously that's not what he teaches in his classes, seminars, to his Gerber baby-like eighteen year-olds from well-to-do families; and just imagine, check this out, get a load of this, the other week, whenever you might be reading or not-reading this, reader, while dis…quisitioning by rote on the Khrushchevean thaw›s literary manifestations and materializations, he completely and mind-bogglingly blanked out on the name, bloody hell, of the author of «One Day in the Life of Ivan Denisovich,» yeah, freaking incredible, really scary, so, of course, he pretended he'd omitted or withheld it on purpose, you know, the author's name, what else could he have done, *bednyaga*, and attempted clumsily to turn the whole thing into some semblance of a teachable moment of sorts, some lame pedagogical ambit, telling the highly unintrigued class to google "The Gulag Archipelago" and let him know who wrote it, feeling more defeated than not, oh that hapless Professor, the poor old former Soviet Jew, run-of-the-mill white settler-colonizing oppressor with a wife and grown son living far away, that old man often waking up in the middle of the night with the routinely comforting thought of, you know, killing himself, in other words, a perfectly normal tail end of life, but... OK, back to Solzhenitsyn, yes, and so the students did as they'd been bid, momentarily animated as they'd been by the minor change in seminar's routine's monotony, freaking Solzhenitsyn, and one of them raised his hand and, in a sudden burst of wholly uncharacteristic curiosity, asked what that odd word, "Gulag," meant, Gulag-Gulag, such a funny word, like goulash or baba ghanoush or something, yes, inquiring minds want to know, and Professor L or simply Professor, yes, again, like in that Paul Bowles story, not Far-Flung Occurrence but something along those lines, told the class then to google Gulag also, google Gulag, yes, google Gulag, he repeated, then again, in his head only this time, google Gulag, gulag Google, such a strange concatenation of sacrilegious alliterations, he thought out of nowhere, apropos of nothing, noticing with distant alarm that he was thinking in words all of a sudden, and not in the ones of his native language either, and feeling unaccountably sad, more intensely despondent than usual, while his disembodied, spectral voice was telling the newly semi-attentive, freshly Gulag-cognizant class something rather incongruous or discordant, whatever the right adjective would be here, pointless, yes, and needlessly inappropriate, to the effect that, well, he happened to like the world of today, where every young person and even newborn babies knew how to google but was possessed of zero awareness of the meaning of the word Gulag, a whole lot better than the gloomy monochromatic world of his own distant beginnings, although in all fairness he had a perfectly normal happy Soviet childhood because childhood is childhood no matter where it unfolds, by and large, in which everyone knew that dreaded word, Gulag, while Google still was light years, as the saying has it, from being invented, and... but OK, this parenthetical aside — aside, my butt, more like… whatever — has gone on for way too long, so let's get back to the main text of this, uh, palimpsest, shall we… shall we… shall we); and so, long story abridged, ooh baby baby, sometimes I feel like a motherless child, ra-ra-Rasputin, lover of midnight poutine, ok, cut it out, it's a whole other story for some other time, Boney M in Russia, and so, with time, as Professor's condition inevitably deteriorated and he grew increasingly more forgetful of words and names and other parts and segments of two languages at once, more mnemonically myopic, if you will (while at the same time, the distance vision of his faraway early memories of his childhood and youth seemed to become sharper, crisper, more focussed… but that, too, would have to be a topic for some other, different telling), eventually every single word in every one of the sentences he uttered would start being replaced with its synonym, alternate, euphemism, what have you, google Gulag, google Gulag, Gulag has no synonyms, euphemistically speaking, OK, fine, and all those synonyms, in their turn, would proceed to generate the synonymic substitutes of their own, burgeoning, multiplying and proliferating, progressively more far-fetched and implausible, whimsically tangential, divergent, and yes, some mornings he felt hopeless to the point of thinking the unthinkable, but why would it be unthinkable to have the soothing and comforting thoughts of ceasing to exist at his age, given his mordant macabre dismal existential situation, OK, moving on, it would be nice to outlive Putin, he thought on occasion, in a purely abstract way, until ultimately he became almost entirely abstruse and even recondite, alas, even to the most patient and diligent and perspicacious of his students and listeners in general, including his wife and his dew friends, all but completely incomprehensible on like a semantic level, a Finnegan's Wake of a speaker, ungooglable like the true essence of Gulag, which indeed cannot be googled, yet toward the end, especially in the last few months preceding his abrupt fall into final stillness, some actually found it rather fascinating, in a limited way, to listen to his, uh, vocalizations, with their sheer whimsical meaninglessness, his fancifully and haphazardly esoteric verbal emissions, as ungraspable as the illusory fleeting shadow of some imaginary giant non-vulturous tropical bird's splendid multicoloured wing's passage, o life o life, google Gulag, google Gulag, a mixture of incomprehensible metaphors, striving to express the inexpressible, forever leaving the shore of the basic shared human understanding and transforming itself into a hermetic hermitic verbal cipher, wholly impenetrable first and foremost to his own disordered mind, a singular matter of extravagant guesswork and elaborate leisurely interpretations, vague surmises, groundless inferences, meaningless metonymies, all grading unmistakably in the heartbreaking direction of nonexistence, just a distant episode of a life thwarted and discontinued, full of senseless symbols and uninterpretable signs, sighs and silence.

24

MAGIC TEA MUG

On my laptop screen, that dastardly portal of pathetic procrastination, a frail-looking old man, seated at what appears to be a breakfast table next to his knowingly giggling grandson (or more likely, great-grandson), is presented — by his daughter or granddaughter, one would imagine — with, presumably, a birthday gift of so-called magic tea mug, which in its nonactivated state looks like a perfectly ordinary monochromatically dark ceramic tea cup, nothing remotely remarkable about it, and the old man, taking it momentarily and semi-automatically into his minutely trembling gnarled hands, contemplating it with an uncertain wan smile of polite incomprehension, OK, it's a tea mug, very nice, but then it is removed gently from his bird-like grasp and a tea bag is dropped into it and boiling-hot water is poured on top of the latter, and lo and behold, the mug's outer surface starts glowing, slowly at first and then faster and faster, shimmering and coruscating, it's magic all right, gee willikers, the old man is gazing in childish wonderment at the black-and-white photograph gradually emerging before his watery eyes, golly gosh gee, he can't believe his eyes, yes, he recognizes it, of course, it's the photograph of him and his late wife in their twenties, one of their seemingly long-lost wedding photos, how in the world, just the two of them, so young and radiant, so handsome and beautiful, so alive with happiness, so full of hope, what a lovely and thoughtful birthday present, aww, he's so very cute, look at him, he is so overcome, he's beyond himself with emotion, such an uplifting moment, and wouldn't you know it, everyone in the room, the seen and unseen ones alike on my laptop screen, is beaming and cheering, congratulations, congratulations, happy birthday, many more returns, whereupon the old man suddenly covers the ravage of his face with his hands and, much to everyone's momentary awkward confusion, commences to sob inconsolably, probably because his life is all but over, it's all in the past for him now, aww, this is so moving and so totally understandable, and he knows that the only really important thing left for him to do in his life at this point is, well, to die, not to mince words, but wait, maybe, conversely, he is bawling his eyes out in an excess of gratitude, yes, that's right, precisely because of the undeniable fact that his life is indeed all but over, for all intents and purposes, all but done, mercifully enough, and soon he'll be free from it, with all its sadness and cruelty, its bodily indignities, limitations and humiliations, these constant debilitating aches and pains, the pesky and downright exhausting daily and hourly responsibilities and obligations of a nominally still-living human being, the sheer crushing *futurelessness* of it all, so damn tiring, he's so damn tired, it's like a mountain, this endless fatigue, and he's so unutterably worn out and wea… but no, what the hell do I know, nada, zero, I don't know squat, so what do I care why he's sobbing, that old man on my laptop screen, let him sob in peace, everyone, for god's sake, avert your eyes, it's none of anyone's business, I've got my own final insurmountable mountain to face, let me waste whatever little time I have left in peace.

25

IINTBEIDNTBE

Some people (no one) sometimes (never) ask me (they don't) why I write these long (not always) one-sentence stories, and I tell them (I don't) that, indeed, apart from the provable fact that more often than not I write the conventional, many-sentence stories, the thing (what thing, everything is a thing) is, when I was just starting out writing in English (a long time ago, a lifetime away, shortly after my arrival in America at age 30), I could, of necessity, only operate with very short declarative phrases and severely limited sets of words, and so now, all these decades later (because life is a process, one that is slow to unfold and quick to come to a close), being able to render a story, however (deceptively) simple or (as if) multi-layered, or even seemingly nonexistent (there are no non-existent stories, although one's life is mainly made of them), in a single 500/1000/5000-word sentence represents (a short word or emphatic interjection might be needed here, in this space, for rhythm-related purposes) a metaphysical victory of sorts over myself in my mind (well, not necessarily a *victory* victory, because what would be the point of repeatedly defeating yourself over the course of your life, but, you know... continually improving maybe, yes, it could be said, on the lifetime-long succession of my metaphorical yet also fully real older selves...

OK, whatever), and it also demonstrates, or illustrates, as though on an imaginary map of my somnolent progress through the years, the… the… the what, the nothing, this is getting boring, I don't know how to explain this to you, IYDKYDK, in internet jargon (there is no such online acronym, LOL, but you, reader, probably will be able to figure it out… and IUDYD), what's there to explain… it measures the sheer ontological (one of those words that mean and explain everything and nothing at once) distance, if you will, that I've covered as a writer (if nothing else) of English sentences (or of Russian sentences in English), but enough, I give up, this is pointless, and as the saying has it, if it needs to be explained, it doesn't need to be explained, IINTBEIDNTBE.

26

HOW TO WRITE A RUSSIAN SENTENCE IN ENGLISH

Let me think about it, since often I never am asked what the difference may be between OK no, if one can write Russian sentences in English, which is an interesting, meaningless and thought-provoking question, if that's what it is, but OK, listen, for instance, in St. Petersburg, Russia, in 2005 (I was born and spent the first thirty years of my life there, in Leningrad, reader, if that's of any bibelot to anyone, by a mother I was born, and my childhood and adolescence were reasonably happy ones, because why not, a childhood is a childhood, one's just biologically predisposed to joie de vivre as a child, but then, at sixteen, like every other newfangled Soviet citizen, I was issued my internal Soviet passport, and from the infamous fifth line from the top of its main page, where one's ethnicity was listed, the word Jew glared or glowered at me, and that started changing my life not for the best in a hurry, although that shouldn't be of any concern to you, reader, OK, just a needless digression), at the end of June, when the pale low-slung boreal sun (accelerate, accelerate) hardly ever disappears behind the vanishing point of the invisible urban whatever, the confluence of water and air perhaps, to put it literarily, during the eighth (I believe) annual international

Summer Literary Seminars program there (it no longer exists, that remarkable and wholly unforgettable something, probably and definitely the most consequential and interesting thing I've ever done in my so-called life, but it's easily googleable still, and I suppose I should let you know, too, ever so humbly and non-braggingly, reader, and yes, Russian sentences tend to be partial even to the weakest of adverbs, that if there is one factoid you should know about me, it would be that I founded that cool undertaking and co-directed it for twenty-plus years, in five countries across three continents, so, I guess I haven't lived totally and completely in vain, and the rest is in my future undertaker's hands), at an impromptu pre-dawn post-boat ride (almost every other night, reader, and here we're abruptly and inexplicably being switched to the third person, coruscating in darkless gloaming, whatever it was I just wrote, a motley assemblage of American and Russian writers and poets of widely divergent degrees of accomplishment went out on the mighty Neva's glorious expanse, see how it rolls, accelerate, accelerate via an intricate network of quaint narrow little Amsterdam-like canals, Peter the Great with a clay pipe in his mouth immediately must be mentioned at this point, to watch those majestic world-famous drawbridges over the world's arguably most literary-centric river being thrown open, one by one, majestically as all hell, cut it out, the viewers' writerly hearts opening up in their poetic chests like so many dangerously enlarged red roses and swelling with... swelling with... well, swelling) party in my rambling rental apartment on Theatre Square (OK, listen, if reading this you still are, there is no such thing as a/the prototypical Russian sentence, obviously, but if you'd like, I could tell you the whole heartbreaking tale of my ill-starred life, one that would make Dostoyevsky himself run out of the living room clutching at his heart, sniffing smelling salts, covered in tears), one of twenty or so of its attendees, an uncharacteristically somber and sober (OK, as a breather in the text, just for the dubious fun of it, imagine *War and Peace* or *Crime and Punishment* written in a single sentence, like Jon Fosse's *Septology* or Tomas Bernhard's *On the Mountain*, reader) young prose writer from your generic California, let's say, whom from hereon in I shall be referring to as JW, his elongated, slightly horse-like, Pasternak-esque face with dark searching eyes gently distorted with what appeared to be some sort of deep inner turmoil, approached at one point the program's honorary guest, a great yet refreshingly down-to-earth contemporary poet from Moscow (he doesn't live there anymore, along with at least one million other Russian people of conscience and other such attributes who'd left Russia, fled it on the spur of the moment in many instances, after February 24, 2022 — in the wake, that is, of Putin's insane, obscene invasion of Ukraine… that singularly, uniquely repugnant bipedal dark hole of humanity, the world's most dangerous man, Trump's master, Musk's guru), just as the said poet and I, standing quietly in the corner of (ah, those, you know, indefinite/definite articles, I'm telling you, those a's and the's and their seemingly arbitrary, capricious even usage in the/no-the English sentences, so wholly alien to any natural Russophone) brightly-lit kitchen and talking animatedly about, say, the sentences we would write if we knew we were about to die, were about to down another shot of vodka, and blurted out (YW did), speaking in a desperately nervous falsetto, the following disjointed sentence, which I am relating here in a willy-nilly Russified paraphrase, OK let's see, "Sir, uh, forgive my interruption, but you're a great Russian poet, a man of profound wisdom by default, so you must be an amazing expert on the intricacies of the Russian heart, female heart in particular, and I'd really, like, value and super-appreciate your advice on my, uh, unfortunate predicament, which is like, OK see, I've met a young woman here, at a nightclub, everyone here knows which one, a few days ago, last week, a very beautiful girl, if I may say so, and, you know, we went out on a couple of dates on two consecutive evenings and I thought those were really good, although maybe I was wrong, that was just my one-sided impression, what do I know, but anyway, cutting to the chase, I fell in love with her, so cliché, I know, but I never felt like this before, right away I knew we were meant to be together forever, but then, ah, story of my life, then suddenly, out of nowhere, she told me, OK this is hard, she told me, OK I promised myself I wouldn't cry, this is humiliating, she told me she, like, could never love me back, not in the way I loved her, unfortunately, never, not in a million years, she couldn't tell me why or what all this was about, but she told me I should leave her alone, forget her, it wasn't me it was her, everything will be explained later, OK I'm not crying, I'm sorry, giving me no reason for her change of heart, leaving me with no hope, just turned around and left, I followed her with my despondent eyes as she was being diminished and ultimately swallowed by foggy distance, and so now I'm at a desperate loss as to what to do, if anything, so please, sir, you must know, I'm sure, what one should do in this situation, what to undertake, what's to be done, please let me know" (incidentally, *What's To Be Done* was, and still is, the title of a cerebellum-numbingly boring ultra-revolutionary mid-nineteenth-century by Nikolay Chernyshevsky, Lenin's literary darling, as a result of which last circumstance we had to read and pretend to digest and discuss that ridiculous idealistic crap with proto-fascistic overtones for months on end in the ninth, or was it tenth grade of high school), and YW's voice trailed off, as he kept staring at the great poet expectantly, longingly, through the invisible Chekhovian tears in his eyes, sobbing quietly, and yes, all this is pretty badly written, I agree, but who said (definitely not anyone I know) that a Russian sentence must be beautiful or make sense, when all it does have to do is keep going, keep going on, keep rolling, almost counterintuitively, despite itself almost, like life itself (life generally is like that — just as you barely begin to understand why you came here, it already is time to leave... a definite bummer), and as he additionally, as an afterthought, let out a thin little cry of agonizing despair, the poor heartsick young American, still staring at the Poet (yes, just the Poet, with the capital P, sure, why not, in the hallowed Russian tradition of such lofty tackiness, as per the late, ever-tasteful and unassuming Yevgeny Yevtushenko's famous dictum, maxim, aphorism that "a poet in Russia is more than a poet"), after I'd translated YW's harrowing words to him, replied curtly and categorically, without skipping a beat, "kill yourself" (pokonchit' samoubiyistvom), causing me naturally to guffaw, give an involuntary chortle of puerile amusement (rather immature of me, granted, but then, on the other hand, I... but oh, come on, give me a break), but since YW was already fairly burrowing into my face with his pleading dark pupilless eyes, and given that I obviously could not possibly, both as a decent and compassionate human being I hope I am and in my official legally-binding capacity of the program director, relate the Poet's harshly sardonic quip to him verbatim (those inordinately sensitive young Western Werthers, the idealistic believers in pure love and the essential human goodness, avid readers of Tolstoy and Chekhov and maybe even Turgenev, finding themselves having been transported as though in a dream to the unspeakable, newly post-Soviet Russia, that, you know, pallid underbelly of the rigid Western psyche, where everything and anything goes and nothing does not go and there are no ethical limits and no moral taboos, the realm of corrosive cynicism, interminable, like the Trumpian "weave," only less moronic, sentences and permanently muddled feelings... yes, my heart went out to poor YW), I told him instead something along the lines of, well, "Look, YW, the Poet basically says that for as long as your aching heart remembers and holds on to the pain of this rejection, the pulsating red-hot flower of a wound in your soul won't heal, and there is no greater desire than that of a wounded person for another wound, to quote Bataille, so perhaps you should maybe, like, you know, just a suggestion, fall in love with someone else, some other girl, look, man, seriously, there're lots of nightclubs in this city, although frankly those are not really the best places to visit in search of true love, which maybe you shouldn't even be looking for anyway while here, in Russia, right now it's not the best of places in the world for true-love seekers from abroad, plus, as we've been telling all of the participants from the outset, those types of places are not entirely safe for foreigners, especially the idealistic and naïve ones, like you, no offence, man, it's a compliment, and you'd stand a much better chance of meeting someone nice instead at the Hermitage, say, or the Russian Museum, some such cultural venue, which I'm sure you know already even without me telling you, but in the meantime, YW, look, OK, have a drink, for God's sake, be young, be happy, be an American in Russia, in this incredible country, an enema wrapped in mystery, in this unimaginable and terribly beautiful and forever unfinished city, and try to think some happy thoughts, my friend, so that's what the Poet said" — and incidentally, as an aside, another quick digression, accelerate, accelerate, I've read an earlier version of this sentence (for indeed, this whole piece in its essence is just an amusing minor episode, nothing more than that, yet one rising potentially to the level of a story due to the way of its telling, by dint of its being rendered in a single sentence, one about Russia and written by a native speaker of Russian, so no, it couldn't just as well have been treated instead in an ordinary succession of sentences, at least not by me, which, in the end, is all that matters) to a group of young writers in Nairobi, Kenya (it's a long story, why I was in Kenya recently, or why I've been coming to Kenya every year, pretty much, for almost two and a half decades now, a whole other story, one for some other time maybe, accelerate, accelerate), and, well, in short, not a single one among those listeners there that night found it funny or even minimally comprehensible, as if I was reading it to them in Russian, and actually that probably would've generated more interest, come to think of it, OK, but perhaps, in fairness, their disinterest was also explicable too, in light of the fact that I'd had a bit to drink that night also, so... OK, the end — yes, thus I spake unto YW, cut it out, who had been listening to me with growing dismay, looking thoroughly confused, and finally, when I was finished, he said haltingly, apologetically almost, that he didn't quite understand how I'd managed to translate the two Russian words, if he'd heard correctly, uttered by the Poet into, like, two hundred or more of mine in English, how that was possible, which certainly was a valid point on his part, and so I nodded and told him in response that, well, you see, YW, in Russian, sometimes a mere single word contains a whole long sentence's worth of meaning and other spiritual components written or vocalized in other languages, like in a zipped hieroglyph of multilayered information of sorts... or something like that, but that by the same token, admittedly, at other times (and this actually was a much more frequent case, I told him) a whole lengthy Russian sentence or large block of sentences could safely be reduced to a mere couple of words in English or some other foreign language or, more fittingly still, to silence, emptiness, white noise of stillness, to nothing at all, yes indeed, if he was catching my drift, I added, winking at him, slapping him on the shoulder, but since he still looked puzzled and somewhat unconvinced, I winked at him again and assured him I was just joking (which I was not, or not entirely), and then we had a drink, and then another, all of us, together and separately, because — oh, Russia, Russia, and my St. Petersburg, good god, I will never see you again, OK well, deal with it, and the gossamer night, glowingly transparent, white-pinkish of hue, wore on lightly into the unworded endlessness of a new day.

27

NO CURE

It's harshly cold outside, it gets dark early, the wind picks up with a whoosh, in a swirl of the biting buckshot of hardened snow, then dies down, as the mutant virus of the second winter of our discontent is haunts the mortified city's downtown core — yet still, the streets are not totally empty, a homeless man on the corner sits down on a lopsided snowbound bench to eat a foil-wrapped sandwich, gives me a cursory, vaguely hostile look, and says off into space, "There's no cure for happiness, brother."

28

NO END

...missing all the places you've never seen, thinking with fondness of all the people you've never met, remembering the thing that never was, feeling nostalgic for the life that could have been.

29

SWEDISH DEATH CLEANING

I was riding a half-empty bus down Sherbrooke Street yesterday, stop, on a grey and windy afternoon, going to my bank in order to deposit a modest check for my recent reading back in the US, stop, I am old-fashioned that way, it's hard to type on the phone on a moving bus, looking vacantly out the dusty window and thinking about someone I used to know and be friends with during the San Francisco period of my American life, stop, period, yes, my life, to put it grandly, stop, in late eighties and early nineties, at the brittle junction of the last two decades of the last millennium, stop, that's just writing instead of an honest reckoning with the way I was feeling, stop, a fellow former Leningrader, who had died the day before, as I'd learned from his wife's post on his Facebook timeline, where else these days, stop, how sad, stop, the straight line of his time in this world had come to an end, he was just six years older than me yet somehow always impressed me as someone naturally belonging to the preceding generation of Soviet Jews, stop, my parents' one, perhaps because of the unwavering fastidious old-fashionedness of his notions about life, the rather reassuring monochromatic moral simplicity, stop, rigidity even, of his unassuming, ever forthright persona, in addition to the fairly basic, strictly functional quality of his English, stop, which last made it inevitable for him to continue inhabiting solely the Russian, so to speak, cultural space in America, stop, as if only his body actually lived in America, and because he was smart and friendly and gregarious and a noted journalist and photographer, he quickly became a prominent member of San Francisco's and, broader, the entire rapidly growing Russophone-American immigrant community, stop, there's no such community as a unified social entity, let's be real, stop, becoming widely known to and indeed to some extent getting to be beloved by many in that large non-community as a prolific, engaging and passionately argumentative cultural essayist and literary critic appearing regularly in every Russian-language newspaper and magazine of note and local and national reach, the author of several books of poignant and evocative interviews with and photo-portraits of such titans of the post-Soviet Russian and international culture as Brodsky, Baryshnikov, Ioseliani, Tarkovsky, among many other such illustrious individuals, stop, that was a long uninterrupted stretch, beautiful, also he published in the US, where else, a beautiful, yes, photo-book on Leningrad, that unbelievable and unimaginable and all of that, wholly unrepeatable city of our mutual first life, our everlasting unrequited love, which neither of us will ever see again, stop, this is just writing again, no, it's not, we would meet often back then, when I lived in San Francisco, to talk at length about literature and writing, stop, life and death and so on, although of course we were two very different people, as I've already mentioned, stop, he was a Republican, of course, though I seriously would doubt he might vote for Trump, no, he hated vulgar people, but he certainly had voted for the Bushes, for McCain and Romney, stop, but we didn't talk about politics, the two of us, and what else, he didn't drink or smoke, loved his wife and his children, loved his life in general, loved living within a five-minute walk from the Pacific Ocean, loved his friends, stop, loved his photo-camera, loved taking photographs and writing about books, loved interesting and admired talented people, I'll miss him, oh I'll miss him, I already am missing him, stop, I think the moral rigidity of his worldview was rooted essentially in the deceptively optimistic ethos of the nineteen-sixties' Khrushchevean thaw, stop, I could explain but don't feel like getting into those epistemological weeds now, not at the moment, stop, one after another they're leaving, as if in a hurry, yes, one after another, it's not even funny, the distant friends, close ones, such integral parts and particles of my life, just being washed away, such strong staccato rain of death, stop, its drumroll on the flimsy tin roof of my life, all of a sudden, or it's like a relentless snowfall, stop, so damn sad, this is truly unbearable, stop, breathe, breathe, stop, he took a rather striking author's photo for my first American book of stories and wrote a lengthy and highly flattering piece about it for a leading Russian newspaper in America, although of course he hadn't read the book, why would he have, he generally didn't read literature in English, at least not for pleasure, stop, then invited me once to a dinner party at his house, down by the ocean, in the Sunset district, upon the said book's publication, stop, some meaningful and recognizable names in attendance were there, the older-generation Russian emigré writers of much prominence, entries into the present and future Soviet literary history books really, stop, and with one of those august individuals I got into a heated argument about, stop, race in America, oh well, old-school, deeply Soviet people, in essence, most of them were, understandably so, or anti-Soviet, rather, which used to be one and the same thing, stop, couldn't really fault them for being who they were, that generation is gone now, and now he also is gone, that good old friend of mine, stop, the latest in the growing list of losses, life seemed simpler with him in it, that rigidly moral and unimpeachably decent and passionately culture-loving man, who looked like a biblical Jew, stop, with those sad luminous eyes of his, so what the hell happened to him, was it cancer, probably, stop, and suddenly someone, in back of me on the bus, a young woman, judging by the sound of her voice, said into the phone, presumably, cheerily, with a lilting laugh, that the person she was conversing with needed a Swedish death cleaning, stop, yes, that's what she said, for if she hadn't said it, I wouldn't have said that she did, as that would've been too stupidly convenient in some far-fetched way, adjusting too neatly to fit in with the random fact of my friend's death, stop, this sentence does contain a story, reader, but it's fictionality lies elsewhere, stop, not on the surface of it, I am a very imperfect man yet I still am better than that, so yes, that's exactly what she said, laughing into the phone, stop, I didn't turn around in my seat to take a look at her, why would I have, I just kept on staring vacantly out the dusty bus window, stop, on the emptiness of the Saturday-afternoon Golden Mile, which is a posh area in Montreal, stop, he was twenty years younger than

Rupert Murdoch, incidentally, that San Francisco friend of mine, stop, and Rupert Murdoch keeps getting married to different people and seems to believe he still is in the clover flush of his early middle age, stop, and then I saw, walking purposefully outside, along the Golden Mile stretch of Sherbrooke Street, almost at the same pace as the constantly slowing-down bus I was on was proceeding, an old or middle-aged man, it's a confusing stage of one's life, in a long lapserdak-like black coat and wide-brimmed black fedora, sporting a nonchalantly trimmed longish beard and round steel-rimmed spectacles on the bridge of his unmistakable nose, stop, in short, in other words, bearing a clear resemblance, at least from the illusory distance between us, to that newly-dead friend of mine, stop, with whom, sadly, I'd fallen out of touch years ago, for no abiding reason, merely because life is the way it is, to put it a bit pathetically, I have no better explanation, we are the way our life shapes and molds us to be, stop, and as I was looking at him, that strange man out on Sherbrooke Street, a visual pang to my conscience, I recalled that just a couple of months earlier, in response to my post of "Happy Birthday, my dear friend, here's hoping our paths cross again in none too distant future" on his Facebook timeline, where else, in Russian, obviously, stop, he responded right away, thanking me and adding, half-wistfully and, I thought, half-reproachfully, "we seem to have lost sight of each other somehow," stop, not an entirely accurate translation, I'm afraid, the ineffable flavour of informal Russian prose has evaporated from it somehow, but what can I do, I am what I am, and life it what it is, stop, and then the bus paused again with a huffing sigh at the yellow light two stops away from my destination, and the man in black out on the street drew level with it, with me, and he turned and looked my way, probably trying to assess the basic advisability of crossing the street at that particular point, from basic safety's perspective, and for a brief second our eyes had met and an uncertain light of recognition flared darkly in his moist almond-shaped soulful eyes, causing me to wonder absently as to what, if anything, he might be thinking at the moment, while looking at me, probably nothing, or maybe that I looked a little like someone he used to know, just some vaguely familiar stranger on a bus staring off into nowhere, still trying to figure out the mystery of it all even in the late evening of his life, stop, and then he nodded at me and half-raised his hand in a passing greeting, and was gone.

30

OCTOBER 4, 1957

I remember remembering being stood up on the wide white windowsill in our communal kitchen in the dark, my mother's hands clasping tightly my pudgy ankles, an always smiling old woman from the room across the endless corridor from ours, crazy Old Alexandra, her toothless mouth gaping terribly in wonderment, pointing up at the sky with her gnarled hand and telling me there was a speedy red dot for me to see up there, called sputnik, also saying something about Archangel Gabriel enormous wings, laughing silently, and my mother telling her sternly not to confuse me with that ridiculous religious gibberish of hers, the window being wide-open into the enormity of the world, the night's still and bracingly cold air smelling faintly of the eternal rot from the dreadful Obvodny Canal, the city's largest open-air sewage artery, people everywhere in our large old apartment building in the roiling heart of midtown Leningrad leaning out the windows dangerously to gaze at the sky and exclaiming joyously, causing me to begin to cry at the heartbreaking thought I had to be the only one in our apartment building and probably the whole giant city of Leningrad who couldn't see it, that invisible red dot in the impenetrable, vast, starless sky, so unfair, then my mother telling me in a conspiratorial whisper she couldn't see it either, instantly making me feel happy in the cozy knowledge that everything was right with the world.

31

WE WILL BURY YOU

One evening in late nineteen-fifties, too long ago for someone like me not to feel just how heartrendingly recent it was (and we're still here, unbelievably enough, and the dark mercury of the Neva waves is still lapping at its granite confines, and Sting, many, oh many years later, in the late fall of the last year of my life in the Soviet Union, is singing "Russians" on a fancy American record bought for an insane some of money from a friendly *fartsovshchik*, google if needed, "we share the same biology regardless of ideology," oh yeah, he's a deep thinker, that Sting, and a friend of mine, a brightly talented writer, is confiding in me in his humble river-bound abode, hole over vodka, of course, that he's in love with the young woman, also a friend of mine, who is in love with someone else, but first and foremost with the idea of leaving the Soviet Union… but I digress), in a single room in a typically crowded and messy communal apartment on the somberly grey and stately Petrogradskaya Side of Leningrad, where the married couple of my then-young (oh very young) parents' friends lived with their one-year-old son, in a nightly news program on the black felt dish of the radio mounted on their wall, the anchorperson quoted, almost in passing, the famous flamboyant existential threat Khrushchev was fond of thundering off to the Western world of capitalism and imperialism, "we will bury you," brandishing his pudgy fist and shaking his cueball-bald head for emphasis — and wouldn't you know it, at that very moment, right after that "we will bury you" on the radio, the aforementioned one-year-old infant, the couple's son, cute as an irregularly shaped button, theretofore sound asleep in his makeshift manger, all of a sudden opened his radiant eyes, gave a peal of lilting laughter and said, distinctly and loudly, "right on," his very first legible words ever, "right on," "vot imenno," in Russian (but we didn't bury it, the West, did we, Nikita Sergeyevich, wherever you are now — no, we first buried you and then Brezhnev, and then Andropov, and then Chernenko... and then the Soviet Union itself instead, so it appears it was us who got buried, rather than the West... but then, of course, the truth of the matter also is, he laughs best who laughs last, as he Russian saying has it, and we can see that the lurid light emitted for the last time eons ago by the dead star of the once-mighty Soviet Union is now, with the delay of turbulent decades, reaching the Western world, poisoning its societal atmosphere and the confused minds of the countless millions of its citizens, yes indeed, just look, for instance, at the veritable orgy of Jew-hatred sweeping it right now, google Andropov and the Anti-Zionist Committee of the Soviet Public, for instance, yes, for instance, and realize that the nominally long-deceased Soviet Union still isn't done with us, not by a long shot), following which he (the baby) immediately proceeded to start crying, probably because he was hungry, which would be a par for the course behaviour for a one-year-old; and of course, his parents, that ordinary college-educated married couple of two Jewish Komsomol (google, if needed) members, stunned initially beyond any human capacity for astonishment by the metaphysically preternatural occurrence they'd just witnessed, a divine miracle as it undoubtedly would have been categorized as anywhere in that hopelessly backward religion-besotted capitalist world of Khrushchev's braggadocious false prophecy, absolutely had to share the wondrous news with everyone they knew and didn't know, every single person they could think of, how their baby had vocally supported Khrushchev threat to the West to bury it, by saying "right on," happily and distinctly and authoritatively, so sure enough, before long, everyone in that Petrogradskaya-Side apartment building and, broader, all across much of the giant city's intelligentsia circles, including my parents, willy-nilly became aware that the wondrous one-year-old in question was some kind of spookily precocious baby genius destined for a life of unimaginably intellectual brilliance… which reputation, though wholly unsubstantiated, alas, by any further empirical evidence in the subsequent course of the boy's physical growth and mental maturation, followed him all through his formative years, his childhood and adolescence and his chaotic youth, right into the still-hidebound early eighties, when he ended up being arrested and sentenced to a substantial prison term for buying five hundred US dollars from a foreign visitor to the city on the Neva — some enterprising gentleman from San Francisco.

32

ONE MORE

Once upon a time there lived in the world a man who, having written over the decades a moderately sizable batch of mildly unconventional and perhaps even potentially semi-timeless short stories, somehow became convinced he needed to produce one more (just one more) of them to round out the fully realized book-length collection that, in his occluded mind, would justify to some degree his lifetime's worth of largely fruitless and frustrating dreams and hopes to be able one day to consider himself, and be considered by others, a bona fide, fully realized writer... and so, wouldn't you know it, he spent the rapidly dwindling rest of his time on earth, up until the clear proximity of the final curtain, in repeated attempts to start and (for god's sake) finish already that elusive last, final story, pinning a scattering of embarrassingly helpless first drafts of it to the cold infinity of cyberspace's indifferent emptiness — and, well, we all know how that story always ends.

33

FINISHING SENTENCE

"Now that my life finally seems to have come to a close," he began, in a hoarse yet still strong voice — and everyone in the room instantly fell silent and listed in his direction, in an appropriately exaggerated attitude of utmost solemn concentration; but when, after an uncomfortably protracted pause, he still hadn't said anything else, one person, perhaps his favourite person in the world, clearing her throat, broke the hushed reverie by uttering timidly in a half-whisper, "Yes.." — and he opened his hooded eyes and breathed in deeply, as if awakening from a trance, and replied with a sheepish smile, "Oh, I haven't figured out yet how to finish that damn sentence."

34

WORDED WORLD

The world consists of worded things, what I have no word for, I cannot understand, and since I know more words in Russian than in English, the world defined by the extent of my Russian is larger than that of my English, yet it also is much smaller, since I no longer live in it.

35

CRYING

A highly literate, sophisticated and articulate literary friend of mine, my fellow former Soviet subject, called me this evening, the second one after the Trumpquake (well, what's there to say, it is a tragic day for America and the world, but life must go on and all that, and unfortunately, it is quite possible for democracies to commit suicide, but life must go on and all that, and yes, there will need to be a lot of soul-searching done on the part of the Democratic Party, a lot of blame to go around, time to wake up and smell the coffee, but life must go on and all that, millions of Trump voters loathe him too, I'm pretty sure, but they loathe the ridiculous excesses of the Left's "progressivist" project even more, yes, it's a debatable point, but life must go on and all that, and yes, Kamala Harris ran the best campaign she could possibly run under the near-impossible circumstances she had been parachuted into, but when an overwhelming majority of the country believes the country to be on the wrong track, well, it just may be too much of the headwinds to overcome, and yes, dark days are ahead, but one must not lose hope and all that, and it is on the bottom of hopelessness that one finds the ground zero of hope and life must go on and all that… and yes, I'm aware as to what Nabokov, for one, thought of dropping even a dollop of politics into a work of fiction, but, you know, although I sure am no Nabokov, I have my own views on the matter, and, with all due respect to him or any other writer living or dead, I write my own kind of fiction), sounding understandably distraught and still residually dumbfounded and disoriented, he called to tell me, this old friend of mine did, that earlier this afternoon, after a few drinks (wine, not vodka… well, maybe a shot of Scotch also thrown into the mix), he took a nap and instantly found himself inside a surreal dream in which, peeking from behind the corner of some massive dilapidated uninhabited brick building with blind, boarded-up windows in an unknown dystopian city, with his heart thumping loudly on the verge of exploding in his chest, according to him, due to a great surge of inexpressible despondency within him, even before he was able to make out any of the basic details of the said dream, clearly nightmarish of nature, that he knew full well he was trapped in, he already knew somehow that he was witnessing, yes, unfolding right before his disbelieving dream-eyes, which were filled with stinging tears, on what clearly was a public execution site of sorts (in the manner of *lobnoe mesto* in Moscow's Red Square, only this one had a different, more, like, rectangular layout… and everything was glitching and shivering there, bathed in drab yellow-sand sepia of sheer otherworldly dolorousness and accompanied in the emptiness of some artificial white-screen background by the steadily crescendoing drumroll straight, wouldn't you know it, out of the pivotal episode of Dostoyevsky's life), the final moments of, yes, uh, Donald J Trump, the 45th, and now also the 47th President of the United States, the freshly triumphant Orange Man himself, who was standing in his typical relaxed and confident posture of a bipedal manatee taking an unhurried dump it its diaper against a rough slab of dark-grey stone wall pock-marked with bullets, with his dark MAGA hat on and in surprisingly little bronze make-up, wearing a sweat-stained white polo shirt that accentuated nicely his sloping breasts and quietly undulating belly, with his helplessly white little hands tied behind his back and a Soviet-era filter-less Belomor *papirosa* (look it up, if curious, my hypothetical reader) stuck in the corner of his tightly grinning mouth with thin colourless lips, staring with contempt and perhaps even a smidgen of pity at a surprisingly and almost grotesquely long line of the firing squad in front of him, at least thirty faceless men decked out in some comically ancient and stylistically incongruous military uniforms and garish high-peaked Hussar's hats, putting one imaginably in the mind of some earlier foreign film adaptation of War and Peace, their bayoneted muskets all pointed at him, Donald J Trump, our morally degenerate dictator (my friend's voice was breaking, quavering on the phone, and when I chuckled, he told me not to, rather sternly, for he didn't find that dream the least bit comical), and then some senior officer, one obviously in command of the proceedings, who theretofore had been standing slightly to the side of that ridiculously long firing line, approached the still perfectly relaxed condemned man, Donald J Trump, who actually seemed to be rather enjoying himself, his back against that slab of pock-marked stone, eyes half-closed, hips gyrating, hands doing his hallmark double-jerk routine, and asked him something, loudly yet unintelligibly, in a language so strangely unfamiliar, it further petrified the suddenly eminently petrifiable friend of mine, an old Soviet refusenik, tough as nails and an ardent Trump loather, although the latter, that renowned polyglot Donald J Trump, apparently understood the officer perfectly and, spitting out the hard-bitten Belomor from his mouth, responded by shouting out, with great force and terrible conviction, that although he'd just won the most historic election in American history, it still had been rigged by the Deep State, and that he, Trump, was the greatest historical character in all of human history, hands down, but as for what kind of music he would like to listen to before being riddled with these dirty-dog traitors' bullets, as a sacrificial lamb on the altar of the rule of law in America, it would have to be Roy Orbison, a very fine individual and huge supporter of his (at which point I interjected, asking my friend how much longer his dream had lasted, because I was kind of getting the point already — or rather, failing to see one... and there was a momentary pause, so to fill it, I shared with him, yes, shared, that today had been a nice day, weather-wise, a clement, unseasonably warm Montreal afternoon, and I had been in my office, preparing for class, and the world, having just undergone a calamitous change for the dramatic worse, from the perspective of at least half of the world's most powerful country and half of the rest of the world), was affecting an unruffled serenity of its surface, yes, and I found that to be so damn sad and even a little infuriating), and so that brusque commanding officer of what seemed to be an insurrectionist army nodded curtly and, reaching deep into the pocket of his roomy dark-green galliffets (there, again, I interrupted my friend's story to inform him that, interestingly enough, the French General de Galliffet had to wear baggy trousers because he was wounded during the Franco-Prussian War, and he was unable to wear tightly fitted trousers in vogue at the time, and so similarly, by osmosis, one might reasonably assume that all the proud top-brass galliffet-wearers in the Soviet Army, especially in the cavalry, also had sustained wounds to their private parts… and also, you know, apropos of something different and less esoteric, all this talk about Trump's electorate's "economic insecurity," the high price of bacon and eggs and such, well, the simple truth of it is that, at least in my opinion, America just is not ready to vote for a woman for President, not now and probably not anytime soon, no matter what, no matter how competent she may be, yes, and even someone like Trump, so demonstrably dim-witted and outwardly vile, will be preferable to her in millions of Americans' eyes, ain't that America, yes, and of course, lots of people in America would happily burn democracy to the ground if the libs get owned in the process, that too is a factor… but please, by all means, do continue with your weird dream), well, anyway, the commanding officer pulled out of the pocket of his dark-green gallifets a smartphone and tapped its screen a few times with his stubby finger, his face coldly inscrutable, whereupon, drowning out the steady drumroll in the invisible distance, Roy Orbison's heavenly suffering voice floated over the dreadful dreamscape, filling and harmonizing it, echoing in the air above, soaring to the sky, singing about how he was all right for a while, how he could smile for a while, but then he saw whoever he saw last night and she held his hand so tight, that person, and wished him well, not being aware of the fact that he, Orbison, would be crying over her, crying over her, in some part probably because she left him standing all alone, alone and crying, crying, crying, crying, oh get a grip on yourself, Roy, as Trump kept shimmying defiantly and doing that obscene double-fisted pumping thing of his (but wait, I broke in again, I thought you said previously that his hands were tied behind his back… oh, never mind), smiling, smiling, smiling ("She would have been a good woman," The Misfit said, "if it had been somebody there to shoot her every minute of her life," apologies, I just remembered that line, but never mind), while that commanding officer was frowning, frowning, evidently displeased with Trump's total lack of visible fear of death, and, again flicking his fat grubby finger over the screen of his smartphone (it might have been iPhone-14, by the looks of it, but I couldn't see it too clearly, my friend said in a quick aside, in his normal voice), he canceled that beautiful song and, beginning to walk back toward the endless line of the firing squad, barked something into the ensuing heavy silence, apparently in the same unidentifiable language, something that sounded like *iahcnok oge atayber* (which, of course, as I realized with a swiftness of the mind generally uncharacteristic of me, surprising myself, was "let's finish him off, lads," in Russian, with words in reverse, yes, Russian semordnilaps… it's a googleable term… but no, my bad, those are not semordnilaps, as the Russian words resulting from the original words' reversal make no sense), and at that unbearable moment, knowing what was going to happen next, my poor friend, the prisoner of that heartbreaking unrelenting dream, tried to cry out "*on, en odan, ehshcul etyebu aynem otsemv ogen*" ("no, don't, better kill me instead of him," again in Russian with words reversed backwards to forward, *non-semordniliapically*... and Trump in reverse, by the way and apropos of nothing, is Pmurt, and I think that would be a better name for him), but he only managed an impotent silent whisper, my poor friend, and thus, unable to wake up and profoundly perturbed as he was by the fact that his dream self seemingly was willing to sacrifice itself for someone he despised and loathed with every fibre of his soul, all he could muster himself to do was to start crying crying crying crying crying over Pmurt, crying crying crying crying over Pmurt, that bastard, yes, for nobody, not even the seventy-plus millions of his voters, loved him anymore, that flatulent blob of rancid protoplasm (the simple truth is, winning doesn't mean you're right, and losing doesn't mean you're wrong, reader), yes, and wouldn't it be unthinkably horrible to keep crying crying crying crying over Pmurt forever, my friend said with a half-sob, half-giggle, how many of us used to cry, inwardly or otherwise, when he won in 2016, but not now, now there're no tears, our eyes are as dry as... well, something very dry, and you just can't imagine, fa la la la la la la la la, how truly terrifying it was, being locked inside a dream about the execution of someone you loathe and despise so much you almost love and sympathize with him, yes, it's deranged not to have Pmurt's Derangement Syndrome, PDS, and this is what happens sometimes when you don't think you're wishing someone to be dead in your mind but your subconscious kind of knows maybe differently, causing you to cry over Pmurt, cry over Pmurt,

Roy Orbison-style, not the way millions of Soviet people of all ages cried and many even subsequently committed suicide (in my Old Bolshevik grandfather's circle, for instance) over Stalin's death and Khrushchev's posthumous denunciation, dethroning, defrocking, de-frenching him), yes, and not the way either how, on the sixteenth of October in 1964, in the lobby of our elementary-to-high school building on Yuri Gagarin Avenue, I saw the school's cleaning woman, *nyanechka* (diminutive of *nyanya*, nanny), which actually was her official job title, crying, crying as the school custodian, I don't remember his name, a nice hard-drinking man, having climbed up a sturdy step-ladder, stremyanka, was removing from the lobby's front wall the portrait of our leader, inconceivably, Uncle Nikita, as we the Soviet children were supposed to call him, what is this all about, *nyanechka*, Arina Rodionovna, tell me, where're our cups, and the morning was characteristically dark and there was snow on the ground, too early even for Leningrad, so I was afraid we were going to be sent back home to pick up our skis for the gym class, for I hated skiing and all winter sports in general, although I was an avid hockey fan and all that, of course, yes, crying crying crying over Pmurt, crying, and how worried-looking my parents were in the kitchen that morning, listening to the stern voice of the radio announcer, I think it might have been the legendary Yuri Levitan telling the Soviet people something that eclipsed in importance even the new great success of the Soviet cosmic program, the triumphant return to Earth of the first *Voskhod* (Dawn) spaceship, Komarov-Yegorov-Feoktiostov, or should it maybe be *Dokhsov*, non-semordnilapically, yes, and mother wondered in a whisper if there could be a war with America because of this now, as she had worried about the sane, only with more reason, a year earlier, when American president was killed, and grandmother, who also was in the kitchen, of course, asked if this was good or bad for the Jews, and... oh, all of a sudden both my old friend and I remembered that today was November 7th, the greatest Soviet holiday, the 107th anniversary, do you remember, yes, yes, good Lord, of the Great October Socialist Revolution, goddammit, do you remember, do you remember, oh yes, yes, and, how, listen, listen, OK, I'm young. I'm maybe fourteen, and it's the Seventh of November, the Revolution Day, and I'm surrounded on all sides by my classmates and schoolmates, the million-strong army of my fellow Leningraders, we're all Soviet people, our entire nation is walking with me, with us, and in back and in front of me, too, and we're walking along the endless Moskovsky Prospekt, toward the Palace Square, where the Great October Revolution of November 7, 1917, took place, in the Winter Palace, the former seat of tsarism, also known as the Hermitage, yes, and is there a placard on a long wooden stick, with the portrait of one of the members of the Leninist Politburo in my hands, yes, akas, there definitely is, and I am not proud of it, it was imposed on me earlier that post-dawn morning, when, still residually sleepy and groggy while standing outside our school building, I was not paying attention to my surroundings, counting crows, as the saying has it, and our school director, nicknamed The Tankist because he had been a tank commander during the Great Patriotic War, in the course of which he had been severely contused and afterwards became prone to terrifying flashes of uncontrollable anger, had crept up on me from behind on the cat's paws of his galoshes-shod feet and told me I would be one of the portrait carriers, yes, it's is the photographic portrait of the ferociously emaciated, ascetic-looking Arvid Yanovich Pelshe, old and gaunt, skeletal, Savonarola-ish, originally from Latvia, whose skull, one can be certain, never once in his extremely long life has been entered by a remotely frivolous, non-Communism-related thought, probably not a single women-related one either, which is why I am not and would never be a member of the Politburo, among many other reasons, but I grudgingly admire him too, his single-mindedness, for instance, and I envy his unimaginable power, yes, although not really, only if someone like The Tankist were to ask me, but in reality I hate and despise the sonofabitch, what a tool, still, long live and all hail to Pelshe and blah blah blah, yes, and of course all my schoolmates, classmates, they're laughing at me, the Pelshe-carrier, and all the girls also, prominently including the one I like, but whatever, you know, I don't care, they can all go to hell, someday they'll be remembering this morning with wistful tenderness, yes, this too shall pass and whatnot, this too shall pass, life goes on, ll the more so that I'm still one of the best players on our middle school's soccer team, plus I'm the captain of our middle school's newly formed KVN (*Klub Vesyolykh i Nakhodchivykh*, "Club of the Cheerful and Resourceful Ones") team, so there's that and it's nothing to sneeze at, yes, plus also, I have this pretty unique, if completely useless in practical terms, innate capacity for spelling every single word in the Russian language correctly, even the words whose meaning is completely unknown to me, even the fancy, long-winded foreign words integrated into the Russian language, lots of those words, a phenomenon of sorts, false modesty aside, I happen to be, in that respect, and in that respect only, well, OK, but so what, it's not nothing, and our teacher of Russian, whom I rather like, because she thinks I'm special, I think, not to brag, has told me not to attend the Russian class, or at the very least to keep quiet during it and try not to correct her in case of her, admittedly very rare, spelling mistakes, yes, and she also thinks I have a future as a writer ahead of me, yes, she even has told my parents so, which has made them seriously unhappy, displeased, and they told her that she shouldn't be putting such silly and harmful and impractical ideas into my head, yes, but anyway, none of that is of any consequence at the moment, because oh, so much happiness everywhere, all around you, although that's not the right word for it, yes, not happiness maybe, but, like, life-affirming roaring, jubilant shouting, and it's a long, very long walk to the Palace Square, or simply The Square, for all of us, this great and still constantly and steadily swelling and multiplying mass of people, more than twelve kilometres, counting from our school building, hours of walking, a veritable lifetime of stops-and-starts, yes, which is why we have set out so early, at seven in the morning, for this walk, for this march, this demonstration, this celebration, o life, o life, how wonderful you are, although it's pretty damn cold too, to be honest, because this is Leningrad in November, a very northern city, close to the Arctic Circe, so will there be a strictly illicit gulp of ersatz port perhaps somewhere along the way, that's what one would like to know, yes, possibly, but not very likely, that would have to wait a little still, perhaps until high school, which is a shame, but then, oh well, how about a stolen, gulp, kiss, somewhere in the confusing narrows of the little streets in close proximity of and leading directly to the Nevsky, huh, well, yeah, right, sure, in your dreams, fool, in your dreams, who do you think you are, pipsqueak, well, fine, but in the meantime, yes, in the meanness of time, closer and closer and closer to The Square we're getting, louder and louder the shouting all around us, the bellowing, the roaring, it's deafening, it's the Revolution Day, the gloriously unforgiving holiday, and now some belated anger is rising in the hearts of millions of Soviet people, and in my little heart also, more righteous indignation against the forces of the international imperialism, against America and the whole dark world of our mortal enemy, yes, and the air is fairly vibrating with our beautiful fury, as we raise our fists to the sky and shout yes yes yes to the familiar slogans being yelled out in metallic voices from unseen megaphones on every street corner and every other tall building's rooftop, it seems, oh yes, Down with American Imperialism, Down with the Cruel World of Capitalism, Down with the Capitalist Exploitation of the International Proletariat, Down with the international Zionism, Down, Down, Down, and down, down, down we shout in return, even if some of us actually are bursting with suppressed laughter, because frankly, I mean, oh come on, down, down, down, while the megaphones keep blaring away, Long Live the Eternally Invincible Soviet Union, Long Live the Unbreakable Brotherhood of the World's Socialist Camp, Long Live the Freedom-Fighting Working

People of Africa and the Middle East, Long Live, Long Live, and long live we shout back at the sky, trying to outdo each other in terms of the loudness and shrillness of our childish voices, laughing, long live, long live, Long Live the Leninist Politburo of the Central Committee of Our Communist Party, the megaphones exult triumphantly, Long Live the International Communist Movement, Long Live the Radiant Future of the Progressive Humankind, yes, and we keep echoing all that at the top of our lungs, long live, long live, long loong looong, loooong liiive, oooh long, haha, long live comrade Arvid Yanovich Pelshe, a friend walking next to me half-exclaims, jabbing me in the ribs with his elbow, which is kind of low of him, since he knows I cannot reciprocate, what with my hands being occupied with Pelshe's haunted mug of a horny eunuch, yes indeed, and the girl I like, who is walking just ahead of us, she bursts out in a peal of giggles, well, OK, fine, have fun at my expense, it's all in good fun, this ribbing, I deserve it too, for having lost my sense of danger earlier in the morning, back in front of our school building, when The Tankist was stalking the perimeter with this ugly thing in my frozen hands, yes, all's fair I love and war, someday revenge will be mine, damn straight, and I smile and tell them I actually am beginning to like him, that poor effer Pelshe, my very favourite Politburo member, he's growing on me with every passing minute of my carrying him, growing, growing, growing, and growing still, he's enormous now inside me, ah, Arvid Pelshe, I think love thee, why art thou Arvid Pelshe, I hate the sonofabitch, I'm going to throw him into the river, that ugly mug, into the free-flowing Neva behind the

Winter Palace, otherwise known as the Hermitage, unnoticedly, surreptitiously, overtly, as if by accident, oops, sorry, I'll make it look as though a gust of wind tore it out of my clumsy hands of a child, yes, that's what I'm going to do, I'm going to do it, I actually am, it's dangerous, I know, and if caught, my whole life will be ruined forever, but what the hell, I'm still doing it, and then I'm going to lie about it, I am, I'm going to lie like a dog, I am, yes, I am, goodbye, Pelshe, goodbye, off into the river you go, yes, and for some reason, for no reason at all, suddenly I feel like crying, and now we are entering The Square and beginning to cross it… crying crying crying over Pmurt, crying crying crying over Pmurt, because our youth is gone, I tell my friend, and now we're old, because we'll never be young again, because our lives are so sadly close to being over, crying crying crying over Pmurt, and I'm looking at the old but oh still so recent photographs of myself with my departed friends, how strong all of a sudden is the staccato rain of death on the tin roof of my life, one after another, one after another as though in a hurry, they're leaving, and there is nothing to be done about it, we've entered this last phase of life, and I feel like crying, but what sense would that make, and there no tears left in my eyes anyway, the past is irrevocable, unstoppable, so there is nothing left to do but to resign yourself to it and be prepared to pull your head into your shoulders when the next blow comes, as the last act of resistance to the entropy of an existence fast gone past, and to keep on living for as long as one's got left, remember us, we had our turn at life, we were here, yes, crying crying crying, yes, someone was crying in the metro this afternoon, after I'd left my dentist's office, after the latter, in the course of a routine checkup, had told me I might need to have a molar removed due to there likely being a crack in its root or some such irreparable circumstance, which would mean there might have to be an implant in my immediate future, to the tune of five thousand Canadian dollars or so, with the extraction, which I wouldn't be looking forward to either, crying crying cying, yes, but sometimes, my friend, sometimes, when light hits you at an odd angle, especially at pre-sunset hour, the golden hour of my life, you feel momentarily happy, like a child, as if you were going to exist forever and were never going to die, out of sadness we live on, to quote Elias Canetti, my friend, I said, oh my friend, *v mehsan etsarzov yns ihsan igarv* — at our age, dreams are our enemies, in Russian, in reverse.

36
THAT GIRL

I still remember someone I met in a dream when I was five years of age and living in the suburbs of Moscow with my grandparents, a girl my age who knew everything there was to know about me, understood me more fully than anyone else possibly ever could, and was the closest person to me in the entire world — and right away, from the very first, overcome with an almost unbearable happiness, I knew with utmost certainty that we would spend the rest of our lives being inseparable, as one and the same person, the most faithful of friends; and she told me she felt the same, even though the two of us had never met in our respective non-dream realities and she would never visit me again in my sleep, it was just that one night in my early childhood, yet I still remember her name and, if a little vaguely, what she looked like, because I kept thinking about her and waiting for her for years afterwards (it is possible, I believe, that many, if not most of us go through life missing someone we've never met, someone we don't even know we've been missing); but now that both of our lives are gradually drawing to a close, I no longer hope to see her again in any of my dreams in this reality, no longer waiting, so maybe we'll meet again on the other side or in another life, Tanya.

37

LIFE HAPPENED

Yesterday, in a rather unbidden and, frankly, a bit of an embarrassing lyrical aside — but an understandable and somewhat forgivable one perhaps also, given the nostalgia-ridden turn of my rambling recollections at the moment, with regards to my self-styled literary beginnings back in since-renamed city of Leningrad, restored belatedly and to a small degree only to the cold grandeur of its squalid imperial essence, the ill-starred city of my life, a thoroughly unlikely metropolis (let's get to the point, you don't have all day… or indeed, maybe you do — and that could be a problem in itself), in equal measure beautiful and terrible, cruel to its heartless brittle core, the erstwhile capital of the senselessly vast old empire hopelessly (too many weak adverbs) lost on its erratic way through the serpentine of centuries and currently, at the absolute nadir of its almost incomprehensibly cruel history, waging an unthinkable and a priori lost war against once-sisterly neighbouring Ukraine and, de facto, life itself, indeed, fighting on death's behalf, excessively literary as that may sound (but the sentiment is real) — I showed the Young Kenyan u (YKW), who was interviewing me for a Nairobi-based publication (yes, I'm in Kenya now, as of this writing, probably for the fifteenth or twentieth or so time in the last quarter of a century, but it's a long story, and I only have — let's see... a little less than an hour to finish this piece here, before leaving for, uh, a meeting, yes, that's right, one with a genuinely interesting person, someone I haven't seen in a good, oh I don't know, eighteen or more years maybe, it's a long story — a native New Yorker from a well-to-do Jewish family who, as a young man, a senior in college, many decades ago, came to coastal Kenya as a tourist, fell in love with it on the spot and subsequently has lived here since, I guess, the early seventies, having in steady order become a near-native Swahili speaker, a writer and esteemed scholar of African history, a philosopher of life, if you will, an entrepreneur and... well, that should suffice, and so, in other words — some other time, about me and Kenya and all the rest of it), a few photographs of myself in my twenties, back in my Leningrad apartment, all by myself, as well as with other people, my college-mates and so on, on my phone, and upon seeing those, YKW started perceptibly, or imperceptibly perhaps, or blanched or whatever, wide-eyed (maybe not), and said, in a carefully hesitant voice, "but... but... what happened," with no question mark at the end — what happened, yes, what the hell happened, yes, what, YKW's involuntary spontaneous reaction implied (and not even implied but spelled out directly), happened to your, well, looks or whatever, to put it bluntly, to your physique, your hair, your entire being, why such harshly glaring and depressing transformation, as if you back then and, you know, the now you were two entirely and completely different individuals (which, if actually articulated, wouldn't have been an entirely inaccurate statement), and also, and maybe even more to the point, what YKW really wanted to know but left unsaid, was, you know, does this happen to everyone, does it have to, this negative metamorphosis, this… well, horror, not to mince the unspoken words, yes, would this happen to me too, me, the lovely and vibrant YKW… no way, no, absolutely not, I refuse to believe it, it can't happen to me, it couldn't, it won't, you just… you, my dear esteemed visitor from afar, professor of literature or what have you, you just must've been somewhat, somehow, how do I put this more delicately in my mind, unlucky, yes, in terms of your genetic composition, something like that, and also, as one might suspect with a high degree of probability, you haven't been taking all that great care of yourself and your health over the years or actually most of your life, that's kind of self-evident, plus you were just telling me yourself about all that drinking you were doing in the company of other underground writers back in your native city, as a young man, and it's clear too that you've never slowed down in that department since, I've seen you drinking too much even here in Nairobi… no, no, I, the lovely and vibrant YKW, for one, will never be that old, or grow old like that, like you have, in the same sad, unattractive way, because staying young, both mentally and physically, is a conscious choice, it's just common knowledge, absolutely a personal choice, a matter of one's priorities in life, and we're not talking (well, we're not really *talking* talking, obviously, but you know what I mean… it's a telepathic conversation we're having) cosmetic surgeries or expensive serums and creams or, like, stupid Botox injections here either, no, no, I insist, silently but strongly, that happiness is as much of one's deliberate personal choice as unhappiness happens to be, trite as that may sound, yes, and… OK, long story short (time is becoming a factor now), I responded to YKW's unintentional unflattering reaction (forty-three minutes left until I have to leave for the aforementioned meeting… which is to take place at a resto in Lavington, and I'm in Nairobi West, and, in case you didn't know, Nairobi traffic is apt to make its LA's counterpart hang its metaphoric multi-lane head in shame), feeling more amused than sad (not quite true, for I did feel a bit sad, but, you know… I'm used to it), life happened, I said, that's what, YKW, that's what happened, life, life, life happened, life happened, that's it, nothing else, and now I'm old, and it's no big tragedy (it is, but it also really isn't), and it happens to everyone, no exceptions, such is the law of the universe, everything that gets born must die eventually, at some point — and towards the end of life, hopefully, if all goes reasonably smoothly and well in the course of one's existence, one just gets old, simply and predictably and unimaginably, no matter how studiously one may be avoiding mirrors or, conversely, be drawn to them, one's heart contracting and sinking each time with stubborn non-recognition of the old person looking dully back from the impenetrable dark depth of its amalgam, one just does, I said, as life, after a certain uncatchable point in time, accelerates on you with a vengeance, and suddenly you're old before you know it and, to put it gently, no longer the joyously immortal child of a lifetime ago, yes despite and totally independently of the fact that when you're little, an infant, a child, a babe in the woods of existence, you absolutely and with utmost positive certainty are convinced that you're never going to die, never-ever, because you're just that special, as we all know, and so on, and then, when you're young, as you are now, YKW, you don't really ever think about getting old and dying either, because why would you, what would be the point, life's way too long for such boring thoughts, you just know beyond the shadow of a doubt that old age won't ever happen to you, screw it, screw old age, you'll stay young and beautiful (the young are always bold and beautiful, regardless) forever, Dorian Greys in reverse, you know, I mean, I'm not discovering any Americas here, YKW, and your face will never get covered with an intricate network of unsightly wrinkles, your body will always remain lithe and brimming and thrumming with energy, your skin will never lose its natural smoothness and, what else, elasticity (incidentally, before I forget, the reason that infernal ghoul Putin, that rabid bunker-bound rat, OK, all right, reader gets the point, I don't like him, so yes, Putin, with his multiple face-altering surgeries and fancy injections with, like, fillers and other such procedures will never use his strategic nuclear weapons, or even the tactical ones, is just that — a man so pathetically intent on forever looking like someone younger than himself, so vainglorious and so obviously afraid of ceasing to exist, is not likely to commit suicide, to call a spade a spade, even by proxy), and at no future point in your life will you come to a terrible, heartbreaking realization (thirty-two minutes left, accelerate) that all of a sudden (yes, it's like a sharp shard of ice entering you heart) you have more friends in the world of the dead than in this one, this temporary home of ours on this Pale Blue Dot, as per the late Carl Sagan, an infinitely smaller one, and that…

but oh well, why even waste time talking about this, we all know we're going to die someday, every single living thing must die in the end, not to beat the dead horse to death (twenty-nine minutes left, time is accelerating on me), but OK, let me just switch the proverbial gears here and let you know, dear hypothetical reader, that right now, as I'm looking out my window and contemplating idly the ceaseless and seemingly chaotic human activity down in the teeming streets and broad avenues and crooked arched alleyways of the bustling Nairobi West area, yes, you, my unwitting accidental co-sharer of this pure miracle of our being fleetingly alive at the same time on this tiny planet hurling through the eternal darkness of the universe, I want to let you know that right now I'm remembering (because memories come in the process of one's writing about having and, indeed, generating and imagining them, especially when under some silly self-imposed time constraint, twenty-four minutes now... still some time left, perhaps in more ways than one) something tangentially related, I believe, to that what happened non-question non-posed to me by YKW — and I'm transposed, no, transported, yes, in my mind to one distant late-spring or early-fall Leningrad afternoon, quiet and serene, with me, a teen of high-school age, a fifteen- or sixteen-year-old, sprawled on my side on the sun-dappled parquet floor of the living room in our family's vividly-remembered spacious (but only by the meagre Soviet standards of the era) apartment on Moskovsky Prospect and leafing idly through the latest issue of Foreign Literature, one of the many magazines my parents (on my mother's initiative) subscribed to, one of the country's most popular monthly *thicklies* (an ugly word, sure, but I don't know how else to translate that term, thick periodicals, book-sized, hundreds of pages), circulation in millions of copies (what a totally different world we lived in then, imagine), just skimming through its contents, my heart beating evenly, rapidly, perennially fascinated as I am by the very notion of anyone's being able to exist (let alone write) in any language other than Russian, yes… and it still strikes me as a little strange sometimes, believe it or not… and at some point coming across, and being instantly gobsmacked by, one particular image in there, a smallish painting by… I want to say (OK, so say it) the Italian communist artist Renato Guttuso, if memory serves me (which it probably does and does not, for that is not its primary function — to provide me with accurate information about my past — and considering that, despite all my concentrated efforts in that direction, I haven't been able to find that image anywhere online ever since), one depicting a grotesquely fat and altogether repulsive and horrifying naked male figure, blood-red, as if it had been skinned alive, sitting in a heavily slouched posture in the emptiness of white-space background and staring dully yet also, it appears, with a measure of smug self-satisfaction at its obscenely enormous distended belly, upon which its short fat little hands are folded in a vaguely Buddha-like fashion and… well, that's what I'm remembering right now, reader, whoever you may or may not be, all these decades later, and perhaps tomorrow I will be better at re-recreating that moment in my aging mind, who knows, it doesn't matter, and the title of that painting or drawing was, quite simply, The Good Life (yes, imagine), and I remember being absolutely floored by it too, some good life, and… well, that's the extent of it actually, for now, and I don't really know why that smallish image in Foreign Literature had affected me so, in such a momentously upsetting way, back then, at that distant instant in another lifetime, a lifetime ago, and why it would continue to haunt (OK, let's be a bit less dramatic, if possible) my memory for years to come, and even unto today, now and then, at random times… perhaps, if I were to give this some more thought, which is what I'm doing right now, it was because somehow, on a decidedly non-cerebral plane, I sensed, or intuited right away, even as a mere teen, that this was not entirely and completely that obscene fat red blob of a man's fault, that hellacious predicament of his, the shuddersome horror of his good life, yes, that he ended up looking and being like that, and that my immediate aghast wonderment as to why anyone, any fully grown adult, would actually choose that kind of good life for himself, allowing himself to wind up looking and being like that of his own volition, that awful crimson-red slab of meat, not entirely his choice and not fully his fault, and consequently, that my instant uncompromising accusatory revulsion at seeing that image might have been at least partially misplaced, you know, due to my excusable adolescent maximalism, for something like that, some version of that good life, could probably, or at least not-inconceivably, happen to anyone, or to many people, as they grew older, for a variety of… well, admittedly, hard-to-fathom, from my perspective of a fifteen-year-old (at fifteen or sixteen, and beyond, I was thin as a reed and effortlessly athletic, weighing between forty or fifty kilos, I seem to remember), reasons, yes, it could happen to anyone, including me, my very own self, possibly, at some point, as my metabolism (a word unknown to Soviet people) slowed … oh no, hell no, no way… oh yes indeed, yes indeed, sure, me too, me too, it could happen to me also, yes, me, whom everybody liked and even loved (yes, a War and Peace reference here, of course, and no, not everyone liked or loved me in my teens, far from it, don't be a willfully idealistic fool, what's with this pretend childlike innocence, faux naiveté, I could be brash and immodest in my excessive verbosity, and besides, and much more saliently and weightily, by then I had already long been aware that the untold millions of people out there, in the unimaginable larger world, everywhere in the vast Soviet land, one-sixth of the worlds landmass, and beyond, everywhere, yes, wanted me dead, disappeared, gone without a trace, sight unseen, the silly little Soviet Jew me… and now we're seeing it again, this worldwide orgy of antisemitism, you're I corrigibly pathetic… I used to think better of you, the world writ large, back in the old Soviet Union), light and agile like Steve Martin's Picasso (OK, cut it out), weighing the immaterial forty-five or fifty kilos (I already said that… I think… no time), capable of executing (and with the greatest of ease, too… yes, indeed, William Saroyan, Jules Leotard… no time, stop wasting time) thirty or forty or, well, however many you might want (hundreds, seriously, with no problem) pull-ups, a truly infinite number of push-ups, fleet-footed fast runner, high jumper, happily airborne, obsessive and (oh, you bet, and how, but that's a whole other story) promising soccer player, yes, me, my deathless adolescent being, with my quick sense of humor, my easy way with words, my loud laughter (nineteen minutes remaining, enough with all this braggado… self-flexing), my many friends and, uh, girls who seemed to like me (enough already, no time, and it's all in the past, all in the past anyway), my… my… I… I… who… who… and yet, and yet… what do I want… life, life… I don't know what I want, I will never have what I want, I will never want what I have, I want to be rid of this humiliating fear of dying, that's what I want to want, life happened, that's what — and since memory, I'll submit to you, has no chronological dimension to it (OK, later, later, and what's there to explain), I am also going to recollect now, in these remaining minutes until the sand of time runs out on this sentence (it's a story, I insist, of course it is, all you need to do to believe me is to imagine me telling all… this to you over a few glasses of wine at some bar in Montreal, imaginably, or New York City) — randomly, though not quite — how, in the next-to-last (or so I believe) year of my life in the old Soviet Union (OK, let me take this opportunity, if that's what it is, to tell you, very quickly, that in the course of my life, among countless other things, I've been a refusenik ⊠ B look it up, if need be, if curious, if you're still reading, if you even exist — for five and a half years, yes, back in the USSR, in addition to having worked as a decidedly mediocre electrical engineer there after college, a thoroughly indifferent semi-secret submarine demagnetizer, that's right, de-freaking-magnetizer, and, finally, on the lowest and safest rung of all of my existential stations, a shift security guard at the Central Park of Culture and Leisure, tasked with keeping a non-dormant eye on Leningrad's only, and the country's oldest, roller-coaster, and… OK, I suppose what I'm trying to say… yes, what the hell are you trying to say, me, I'd also like to know… is that mine has been a fairly long life, and that it happened, it surely did, my life did happen, for better or worse, in all the quiet, hushed, minorly consequential non-glory of its relative insignificance, yes, I am a modest man now, life has happened to me, although it hasn't been a total waste, my life, I'll submit to you, it hasn't been, and I suppose it still keeps happening, too, in a manner of speaking… I mean, I'm still alive, in the same manner, and I'm writing these words… life did happen to me), how, one late afternoon (oh, me and late afternoons, you know… we go way back), while waiting in a sinuous long line in front of a liquor store on Chernyshevsky Prospekt, diagonally across from the unlivable, condemned and depopulated Dostoyevskean (yes indeed, you guessed right, I'm just using that exhausted, empty non-word out of the perverse subconscious desire to annoy myself, bear with me) apartment building, in the rooftop mansard space of which the so-called westerners wing of the semi-unofficial, underground, samizdat literary club I belonged to at the time was located (and there's much too much context here for me to be able to adequately explain even a small part of its entirety to you now, especially under this self-imposed time constraint, so… OK, well, I'll just have to leave it unexplained, I suppose… all the more so, incidentally, since I've already written about it, that's right, in an old sentence-story, more or less like this one, only shorter and tighter, more compact, called Sentence, which is googleable, it's online and easy to find, if I can be shamelessly self-referential for a moment), and I was passing the time in that line by conversing casually (no, formally… stop wasting time) with an old man standing right behind me, with a face as narrow as a knife blade (not a terribly original description, I know, but… no time), telling him, among other extraneous things, that I was about to celebrate, with my literary (eyeroll) buddies up at the top of that there condemned building across the way (I waved back nonchalantly in the general direction of… OK, fifteen minutes left, damn, hurry up) my, you know, translation of this American writer Guy Davenport's short story *President Richard Nixon's Freischutz Rag*, that's right, Freischutz, no clear idea what that German word means exactly, old man, just as much at a loss as you are, although that's not true, it has something to do with freedom, yes, which is about Richard Nixon and Henry Kissinger in China, on that historic visit, the story is, on its surface, visiting Mao, and it has this extremely cool nonlinear or whatever structure, separate segments of differently accelerated and stylistically rendered text spliced together, and also about Leonardo da Vinci inventing the bicycle, a pretty pivotal moment in human history, in the real time of his life and our reading, quite the juxtaposition, comrade, and it's true, we can't help reinventing that bicycle, can we, the human race, as well as it's about Gertrude Stein and Alice Toklas, don't know if those names say anything to you, it doesn't matter, drinking wine and chatting and getting drunk in Luxembourg Gardens in Paris, where neither of us has ever been, old man, so the story essentially is in its form, the mode of its construction, the way it's laid out, its structural arrangement, from light to darkness, from hope to, you guessed it, hopelessness, like (hasty, sloppy, hurried writing, reader, granted, I recognize, but… no time, no time), OK, comrade, listen, the story is too beautifully conceived and, like, imaginatively narrated for me to be able to do it justice retelling it for you right now, but anyway, that's the gist of it, so… and so, already giddily inebriated, of course, I was blabbering away at him, that old man, who was listening and nodding, nodding and half-listening, his face inscrutable, silent until, during a second's pause in my stream of words, he opened his largely-toothless mouth and, well, shared with me the suspiciously literary-sounding story (but I didn't care then whether it was true or not, and I certainly don't care now) about how, ever since his having been rehabilitated and released from (where the hell else, given his age and the characteristically otherworldly, semi-biblical or something severity of his countenance… no question mark needed here either) the Gulag camp in 1956, the year of our (yes, our) invasion of Hungary (and now, inevitably, it's us, all of us, in one indirect way or another, indeed, because of our shared and even not-shared past, trying to annihilate Ukraine and every last remnant of goodness within ourselves as a non-existent nation, it feels like, although I've sling ceased feeling like I do belong to it, our entire hopeless former or present nation made up of all those whose life or at least its beginnings transpired, if that's the right word to use, within the ambit, ditto, of Russian-Soviet cultural space… although I know that many people, myself possibly included, may think that I'm full of shit, and maybe I am, but I don't think so, because that's just how I feel, and there's no arguing with… no time, no time) and the

Melbourne Olympic Games, among other memorable events, such as Khrushchev's throwing Stalin's blood-drenched spirit under the hopelessly slow and antiquated bus of history, he, that old man, mysteriously lost the ability to see his own reflection in the mirror, that old man, indeed, reader, like a vampire, not that I want to be disrespectful to any Gulag survivor, and so, he told me, for himself he was a man without a face (Putin is a man without a face, too — sure, let me waste a few more precious seconds of rapidly dwindling time on this earth-shattering observation also — as the dead-fish-eyed ghoul jettisoned his previous non-faces repeatedly, one after another, due to his fear of getting older and dying, as if looking younger could prevent one from getting older and dying, so was he casting away also his previous non-lives, so in that sense, his life has not happened, as none of his successive non-face no-faces reflect or testify to time's passage, for a man without a face is a man without a life that has happened to him... but then, what do I know), and there was a strong liberating factor in that, too, he said, the old man, although he didn't use the word factor (but we spoke Russian, so who cares), in not ever being able to see his own face, it made him feel free from himself, he said, seeing my face and other people's faces was plenty enough for him, maybe he used the word element, and (pre-empting the question that... well, actually was not on the tip of... no time) it was his niece, he said, his late sister's daughter, who came to his place, his small room in a permanently messy and routinely overcrowded communal apartment midtown, twice a week to give him a shave and such, generally to take care of him, without fail, and he was very glad she was there for him, because it was important to him somehow to present to the world the appearance of, well, OK, an old and inwardly dead man that he was, sure, yet also one still with his dignity and most of his faculties intact… and overall, he added, rather inconsequentially, I thought, while our birth is totally random from our perspective as fetuses and seems like a miracle each and every time, our death, on the other hand, is natural and unavoidable, beautifully and rigidly predetermined, we know it will come, there's no avoiding it, and there is comfort in that, a great deal of relief, the way I see it, he said, yes, young man, I really look forward to it, to not being around the living anymore, I feel like I'm in control of my life in that way, and let me tell you, I'm grateful for not having made more terrible and irreversible mistakes in my life, apart from and in addition to having been born where and when I was born, I wouldn't want to relive my life, that's for damn sure, yes, at which point I kind of started losing interest in him and his abstract utterances, all the more so that we were already practically at the liquor store's entrance, so I said to him, just in order to say something, that, you know, no matter what, in spite of everything, all the horrors he'd gone through, his life had happened, oh yes, it sure had, so he shouldn't be too hard on himself, the past was past, as Chairman Mao told Richard Nixon in that Guy Davenport story (eight minutes left, it's full-on race against… time, time), to which he replied, in a tired voice, barely a whisper, that he used to wish, back in the camp, that he could go back in time and start life from scratch, everyone has dreams of that nature in times of hardship, but then he realized that it probably and almost certainly would have been even more of a nightmare, an even worse life that than the one he presently was finishing to have, in which he was talking to me now, a total inconsequential stranger and fellow drunk, for there was no cheating fate and instead of doing the mercifully short ten years of burrowing into the camp's permafrost, he might very well have ended up being shot in the back of the head with an NKVD bullet on some gloomy outskirt of Leningrad, his dead body falling into a hastily dug (by the soon-to-be-dead themselves) shallow mass grave, subsequently to be covered with layers of lime and earth, and that would've been a worse outcome for him, he believed, because life was always preferable to death, even when it clearly wasn't, as happened to be the case with his life at the present moment, yes, and so, he added, looking up at the overcast, low-slung Leningrad sky with unseeing eyes, we're stuck until we die with the lives we've been meant to have, young man, for better or worse, till death do us part with ourselves, yes, sure enough, we could've lived very different lives perhaps, under a very different and more benign set of circumstances, but that didn't happen and we ended up having the lives we… we… and oh, reader, I've just remembered, out of the blue, this Aldous Huxley quote from somewhere, for no reason, just a second, let me try to… how am I doing on time, OK, no time, OK, something about its being dark because one's trying too hard, so one has to learn to do everything lightly, feeling lightly even though one's feeling deeply, just lightly letting things happen and lightly coping with them… yes, beautiful, isn't it, and believe it or not (that would be entirely up to you… OK, stop wasting time), the next thing I knew, the old man, all of a sudden, without finishing his sentence (as I'm about to start finishing mine, this one… five measly minutes left), turned, you know, totally ashen, as they say in works of literature, and, just like that, started listing to one side, in the manner of a sinking ship, then slowly and quite terrifyingly fell down onto the Prospect's uneven dirt-spattered asphalt, like a human building being demolished, causing, needless to say, a certain amount of momentary havoc, some anxious rippling and uneasy stirring all along the line of the hungover souls, yes, and someone (not me, I'm sorry to say… I just stood there, stunned, staring at his prostrate body, he still seemed to be breathing) shuffled off to the nearest phone booth to call the ambulance, *skoraya pomoshch'*, which last arrived with commendable swiftness, and… well, I have no idea, obviously, what happened to him after it took him away, that old man with a knife-blade face who couldn't see his own reflection in the mirror, so we'll never know whether he lived a little longer that day or died on the way to the hospital, it doesn't matter, either way would've been fine by him, the world writ large wouldn't notice his disappearance (although his niece, for one, would), yes, his life, having happened, had come to its conclusion (three minutes, OK, one must honor one's own self-imposed constraints, I'm typing as fast as I can, I'm not a fast typist, to put it mildly, I type with, let's see, three fingers, I suppose, four maximum and almost never, I'm just afraid of or rather averse to putting a full stop at the end of a sentence, maybe you or someone you know can relate to that, this piece has no overarching theme or any special meaning, although maybe it does, I would kind of hope so, but that's not for me to judge, so there will be no so-called coda to it, no always-be-closing and all that type of nonsense, no closure), that old man, that old man, life happened, life happened, life keeps happening (if, for people like me, those of my age and my past, it is doing so at a markedly and naturally slower pace at this point, with a steady deceleration, that's just the way it goes, life, life), and... well, OK, finally, let me tell you very quickly that I've just remembered (I should stop remembering things, at this point, I know, but, well, what can I do, everything reminds me of something else) watching online the Muhammad Ali memorial service in Louisville, KY, back in... OK, 2016, yes, that I remember, and how, as Bill Clinton was speaking, eulogizing, fighting back tears, yes, Bill Clinton, Muhammad Ali, two world-famous people, I was thinking, with light sadness (oh wow, a giant marabou stork, the angel of you-know-what, OK, stop it, no time, flapping its enormous Marquezean wings majestically, cut it out with all these random references, just flew, blotting out the sun for an instant, right over the roof of the unprepossessing yet fairly tall and not even remotely condemned or unpopulated building in Nairobi West, where I'm sitting in a small top-floor apartment, looking out the window, thinking and remembering... life happened, life still keeps happening... no time, no time), so OK, yes, I was thinking at that moment of the perfectly ordinary, unremarkable, unknown to the absolute majority of the human race, lonesome old woman, ill, infirm, limited of mobility, my mother's closest friend since high school, who had been kind and nice and funny and easy with a laugh and truly, strikingly beautiful even in her middle age, yes, god, was she ever, and starkly and incomprehensibly unlucky in love, childless, and in general someone who'd known little happiness in life, as life kept happening to her at the wrong time and in the wrong place, Leningrad, Soviet Union, being Jewish certainly didn't help, and now the tsunami wave of antisemitism is rolling all across the world again, for the second time in my life... OK, no time, no time... and who had died, that old woman, the day before Muhammad Ali's funeral, in St. Petersburg, Russia, at eighty-six years of age, just one of more than however many tens of billions of people who had gone that way before her, before you and me, before some of my dearest friends, and now my mother is also dead, but no, no, I won't, and I . . .

38

GRATEFUL

I am grateful for the people I love and for the people who love me in my life; and I am grateful for knowing that people who love me and all of us do so because it is they who are good, not me, not us; and I am grateful for having the capacity to feel and to feel alive; and I am grateful for having crossed paths and broken bread and held hands with many people in my life; and I am grateful for all the good and kind people in my life; and I also am grateful in a way to the bad and hard-hearted people in it also, for having inevitably been a part of my life; and I am grateful for having been given a life and grateful for its still continuing; and I am grateful for still feeling like keeping on living and still being able to hold on to some small private sense of purpose in it; and I am grateful to life for making it so that sometimes it is just when I touch the very bottom of despondency that I find myself being filled with the glowing light of gratitude, and that it is the cold darkness of hopelessness that always, even now, strengthens my resolve to look for hope in life.

ACKNOWLEDGEMENTS

Without the love of my loved ones, the steady friendship of my friends and the goodwill of good acquaintances, the kindness of my readers, and the patience and wisdom of my editor, this book would not have been possible — nor, indeed, my very life as it is known to me. Feeling grateful.